The Grey House DC

The Grey House DC

DUKE TIPTON

iUniverse, Inc.
Bloomington

The Grey House DC

iUniverse books may be ordered through booksellers or by contacting:

iUniverse
1663 Liberty Drive
Bloomington, IN 47403
www.iuniverse.com
1-800-Authors (1-800-288-4677)

ISBN: 978-1-4697-4636-4 (sc)
ISBN: 978-1-4697-4637-1 (ebk)

Printed in the United States of America

iUniverse rev. date: 04/20/2012

CONTENTS

THE GREY HOUSE DC
INTRODUCTION

The Grey House DC story is fiction. Some of the situations in this book are real. The Author took his literary privilege and massaged the facts into a story that should not offend anyone. Most of the elements of this story are recorded in the syndicated newspapers and popular slick cover magazines.

In order to be elected President of the United Stated of America, officially, several conditions must be met:

1. You must be fifty-one years old or older.
2. You must be the favorite candidate in your political party.
3. You must be nominated by your political party.
4. You must win your party's nominating vote.
5. Most of all you must have access to lots of money.
6. You must win the national election over your opponent.

Unofficially you must like to party.

This book describes some of the goings-on during these processes.

This book takes you into the inter offices of the Executive and Legislative branches of Government.

THE FUND RAISING PARTY

Thomas Epstein and Daniel Bachlor were sitting next to each other in the comfy little booth at Dhalis's restaurant. Tom was there with his wife and Daniel, an old bachelor, was there alone. They were fast becoming best friends, with Tom as the new person and Daniel taking him under his wing as the incumbent. They were in for a long road ahead together, running for the House of Representatives. It was a lot of work and Tom felt like he was always under the spotlight, but he was cut out for being a politician and even enjoyed the fierce competition. There was a lot of pressure, and Tom did well under pressure. That is part of why Daniel liked him so much. The kid simply had spunk. There was still a lot he had to learn about what it really meant to be a politician and get involved in "politics" but Daniel was more than happy to show Tom the ropes. After all, Tom was a great person with impeccable morals. He was trustworthy, and kind, if not a little too straightforward. They were eating out together so that they could relax a little before the two men had to go to a fundraising party for the both of them.

As seven o'clock rolled around, the two men decide it is time to get going. Everyone has finished his or her meal and Daniel graciously picks up the bill. Daniel comes from a wealthy family of old money, so a small bill at a cozy little diner is no big deal to him, although Tom and his wife thanked him as if it means the world to them. Dan knows that they are just being polite. Tom's wife, Linda, takes her minivan, and the kids, home, while Tom hops into Dan's Mercedes. Dan keeps telling Tom how he needs to get a new car, something that says smart and classy, like a Mercedes. Politics is all about image. They drove off to the fundraising party, gossiping about this and that. In the car, Dan decides to give Tom a few pointers for the party. "OK Tommy boy, this is a big party, a lot of money is going to be at this shindig. Lots of old widowed women and battle weary old men. Remember to listen more than you talk. The best thing you can do is get on people's good sides by letting them think you are interested in them. However, the real secret to getting money at these parties is in the old lonely women. They do not tell you this in grad school or in your summer internship. However, a good-looking young person like you should have no problem fundraising. The old women pretend that they are high and mighty, fighting to save the world and all that, but really, they are just lonely old women looking for a strapping young man, like you, to come along with whom they fantasize. You have to play to their imagination.

Tom just sat back in his seat and nodded. He knew what he was getting himself into when he signed up for this job.

Tonight could be a rough night, but he was going to drink a lot. Tom had the good fortune of being able to hold his liquor very well, so that he could turn almost any boring or tedious task, such as tonight's fundraiser, into a good time. Moreover, not all fundraisers are filled with old women, for lots of them he has to chat with politicians' young daughters, and proud single independent women who tend to show up at the fundraisers so they could feel important by donating money.

Tom's wife had gone home with their two kids because, although many of the fundraisers require the presence of his family, to show the kind of all-around-good-family-man that he was. However, swankier events such as this one were supposed to only be for men and women involved in the active political scene. This was because these kinds of parties always ended the same way. People paired off to go into separate rooms and areas of the building to trade favors. Usually these favors were exchanged for a donation to a specific campaign or political party.

Dan pulled the car up to the building where the fundraiser was being held. This big old building was almost exclusively used as a gathering place for big events or fundraisers. They both got out and the valet took the keys to go park the car. They were both dressed up nicely in fancy suits and walked into the building with a swagger. This was not a dinner function or an auction, but just a gathering of people. There was some light music playing as they entered the main hall where everyone was gathered into small groups chatting. It was early, so the place was not packed yet. They did not see anyone they knew right off the bat, so they walked over to the bar together to get a drink.

Dan was a drinker, but drank far less them Tom did. Drinking was just another part of the job for Dan. Drinking was something social, not really something he did for pleasure or releases. Not the way Tom used alcohol. Tom ordered a scotch and water. Dan ordered a rum and coke. They sat at the bar and looked around the room as they downed their drinks. Dan noticed an older woman who he knew from a rally he once attended on public school reform. He motioned for Tom to follow him.

A big part of Dan's job was to be a mentor and guide for Tom who was new this year to the campaign. So gradually, the two went everywhere together and spent a great of time together. They had just become friends when they met a little over two years ago. Since then, their friendship had only grown into what must be called brotherhood, despite the lack of familial relations. Although there was a fundraising party for the Presidential candidate going on at the same time as the Congressional fundraiser, many of the contributors attended both parties. Seated at a table near the bar was one of the largest political fund contributors of all times, Bulla, moneybags, Klinginghouse.

Both Tom and Daniel walked over to her table as soon as they saw Bulla. After the normal introductory pleasantries, Daniel asked Bulla whom she was routing for this election. Bulla said, "The best man of course." Daniel said, "Well you know me I am no angle but I would like for you to get to know my friend here, Thomas Epstein. He is the most trustworthy, honest, and straight shooting fellow you could ever meet. Many of his political views match yours right down to the wire. Tom was born on a farm and you know those people just do not have a lot of money.

Now Bulla I know you have been very generous in the past and believe me every penny was appreciated, but poor old Tom sure could use a little pocket change." Bulla responded, "You know Daniel I am only giving out ten grand checks this year. This has not been a good year for me. If you can use ten grand I'll write you a check right here." "Here Bulla, Here's a pen." They both walked away with a ten grand check each.

Tom and Daniel returned to their stool at the bar. Daniel told Tom that one of the best bets to get money at one of these things is to get friendly with the lobbyist. Many of the lobbyists are here with their clients and they have their fat wallets with them. You must do a little research first. You must know what the client wants. You must have a plan to give the client what he wants. Usually the plan is nothing more than you telling him you will tack on to an appreciations bill a rider giving the client his desires. Daniel looks around the room for some familiar faces. He sees a woman setting alone that he had never seen before. She is giving Daniel the eye. Daniel tells Tom, "There is a couple of grand setting over there all alone. Let us go check it out." As they approach the women's table, Daniel said, "Pardon me madam, may I introduce myself. My name is Daniel Bachlor Congressman from second Congressional District. This is Congressman Thomas Epstein from the west coast. What brings you to a political fundraiser, may I ask?" She said that her late father was a politician and he always brought me to the fundraisers and I do it out of respect. Besides, you get to meet so many nice people at the fundraisers. Daniel said, "Well lady I don't know how nice we are but we are here trying to raise money to keep our seats in Congress." She said, "I usually give a couple hundred unless I get to know you real well." Daniel said, "Just how do we get a good acquaintance started up so you can know us real well?"

She said, "Well big boy you could come over and sit by me and we can talk about it." Tom said, "If you will excuse me I think I'll get another drink."

As soon as Daniel sat next to the woman, she put her arms around his shoulders and turned a quarter ways around to face him. Her knees wound up between his legs. She said, "I think I could go for you in a big way Mr. Congressman." He replied, "How big of a way in dollars." She said, "If I exchange money for love that makes me a you know what. Why don't we go to a motel and talk about it, huh, big fellow?" Daniel said, "Why don't you make a generous contribution and then we will talk about a motel?" The woman opened up her purse and pulled out her checkbook. She said, "How much do you think you are worth big boy?" Daniel said, "Anything with three zeros behind it." He put the check for five thousand in his pocket and off they went to the nearest motel.

When Daniel came back to the fundraising party from the motel, he saw Tom with two old women. They were laughing and punching on one another. They told Tom that they would like to play around a little bit. That is all nothing more. One of them said, "If you take us to a motel we will give you a ten thousand dollar contribution. The two women must have been in their 80's. Tom decided the two women could not do him any harm and ten grand is ten grand. Tom said to Daniel, "See you later alligator" and left with a woman on each arm.

When Tom came back to the fundraising party, he found Daniel at the bar talking to three old women, they each had their wallets out of their purses. It appeared that they were discussing the amount of their contribution. Daniel collected some money and the women left. Tom came up to Daniel and said, "Daniel, don't you ever tell Linda that I was out with two strange women. She would not understand at all. So please keep it quiet." Daniel said, "Sure pall." Daniel asked, "Well what happened buddy?" Tom said, "One of the women said we'll give you one grand to see you completely naked. Therefore, I took all of my clothes off and they gave me ten one hundred dollar bills. Then they wanted me to lie in the bed on my back. One of them began to kiss, lick, and slobber on my chest. The other one just stood and watched. They both kept their close on all the time I was there. They gave me five grand in hundred dollar bills. They would not let me dress myself. They put all of my clothes on for me. Each one gave me a brother-sister type kiss and they left. Well anyway, I am sixteen grand better off than before. Daniel said, "Tom, I think you are going to make it."

Daniel suggested they go to THE GREY HOUSE DC and see how the Presidents fundraiser was going. As soon as they interred the building, guess who was seated at a table near the bar. Old money bags herself, Bulla Klinginghouse. Daniel walked up to her and said, "I thought I saw you at the other place?" Bulla said, "Yes, you did and you got twenty grand of my money." Daniel said, "Well we came here to see if we could get a little bit more." Bulla said, "It's not fair to hit a girl twice in the same night. You guys just run along."

Daniel and Tom did a quick tour of the place hoping to find a wealthy target. There was lots of money there but only the high rollers that the President attracted. Daniel and Tom decided to call it a night and go home in Daniel's Mercedes. Just as they were leaving one of Daniel's fellow members of the house finance committee said, "Hey, Daniel I have someone here I want you to meet. He introduced Miss Hanna Louise Steudapekker. Hanna is not a registered lobbyist or even a lobbyist in the strictest since of the word. Her activities might make you think she was a lobbyist. Hanna used to be the head nurse at a 1200 bed cancer hospital on the East coast. The patients at the hospital loved Hanna, no it went even further than that, and they worshiped Hanna. As head nurse at the hospital she would often wheel a terminally ill patient out to the greenway and supply a stick of marijuana. There was no curing effect in the drug but it did ease the pain. One day the security guard caught Hanna supplying the marijuana to a patient and reported her to the hospital administrator. Hanna was relieved of all duties at the hospital and her employment record was permanently damaged. Hanna assumed the leadership in the imitative to legalize medical marijuana. She has played a major role in this initiative. Many of the Medical organizations secretly supply Hanna with funding to help this cause. Several Doctors have contributed to the effort to legalize medical marijuana. It is rumored that Hanna has over seven million dollars in a Swiss checking account to fund the legalization effort. Daniel told Hanna that there was already a bill before the house to legalize medical marijuana. If this bill fails, I personally will introduce another similar bill. Hanna asked, "What kind of expenses do you expect your effort will amount to?" Daniel said, "Well if you count the gifts to help the vote along." Hanna interrupted, "Yes, count the gifts, count everything." Daniel said, "One million should cover it." Hanna said, "Daniel, I will electronically transfer one million dollars to your account first thing Monday morning."

The President held several more fundraising events all of which were great successes. The opposition only rose only about one quarter of the money the President was able to collect.

THE PRESIDENTIAL CAMPAIGN

With enough money in the bank for a first class election campaign the presidential candidate struck out for Alaska and then on to Hawaii. He was making speeches, shaking hands, kissing babies, and promising all sorts of things he knew just cannot be done. He hired a very capable campaign manager. The campaign manager accompanied the presidential candidate but was constantly on the phone with campaign headquarters. The campaign manager had spotters out in the audience measuring the voter reaction to every word the candidate said. The voter sentiment towards each speech was recorded and passed along to the speechwriters. The theme of each speech was adjusted slightly to conform to that particular audience's desires.

Soon it was backing home for some more hand shaking and baby kissing. The campaign manager arranged for a grand whistle stop tour by train. The campaign manager could not rent or lease a train so he just bought one. A cross-country train trip was exhausting. The return trip was by motor coach. The manager purchased a 40-foot long completely self-contained Travelodge motor home. They did have a little trouble finding campgrounds that could handle such a large vehicle especially in the rural areas. When in the big cities the candidate wore a three-piece business suit, white shirt, and neck tie. In the rural areas, he wore blue denim overalls. In the coastal areas, he wore a swimsuit. Our candidate was very flexible. He adjusted to the occasion like a camellia.

The campaign day started at 5:00 AM and lasted until past midnight. There was no need for sleeping pills as everyone was completely exhausted at bedtime. They carried their own chief as mealtime varied to fit the speech schedule. A scout was sent out to case the scene and to make certain that the major political leaders were introduced to the presidential candidate. In the major cities, the presidential candidate would ride the trolley car or the city street bus. When the campaign was over all of the women and babies were kissed, and all of the men had a vigorous handshake. When his wife met him at the bus terminal he said, "I'm sorry honey but my kisser is worn out."

On November election night, it became obvious that our man had won at about 9:00 PM. The opposition conceded at 10:39 PM. In his concession speech the opponent said, "Although there are major differences in our philosophies the new president-elect has a fierce dedication for the letter of the law.

ELECTION CELEBRATION PARTY

With his shirt collar unbuttoned and the neck tie loosely around his neck, the president elect raised a Manhattan cocktail and made the following profound announcement, "The best news I ever heard in my life was the news-caster saying, 'The opposition has capitulated'. It is time to party. Let's party guys." His tinseled red party hat on his head the president elect began to shake the hands of all of the male guests. He gave each female a big hug and a friendly kiss. After hand shaking and kissing over one hundred people the president elect stepped to the podium and began to speak, "I wish to thank each and every one of you for your winning effort. I could not have done this without you. Again thank you. Thank you very much." Someone snuck up behind him and poured a bucket of cold beer down his back. The president elect said, "Oh, that's cold. Now let's let the good times roll."

The President and his party were all smiles and light hearted over the victory in last November's Presidential election. The President was a very successful fundraiser. He did not need, nor did he accept the matching Federal funds. In fact, when the final accounting was over, the President's war chest was 2.6 million dollars to the good. One of his cabinet members, a very close friend asked, "What are you going to do with all of that money?" The President responded, "Throw one 'whing-ding' of a party of course" Two days later the President called Lori-Ann Carlson, the GREY HOUSE, DC, Events Planner, into the circular office and said, "Lori-Ann, How much of a party can we have on 2.6 million Dollars?" Miss Lori-Ann said, "One of the biggest ones that The GREY HOUSE DC has ever seen, Mr. President." The President said, "Lori-Ann I want you to start planning a 2.6 million dollar Celebration party. Think you can handle that?" Lori-Ann responded, "Sure thing Mr. President." The next few days Lori-Ann spent contacting food venders and entertainers for possible party slots and gigs. Each contact was asked to give a cost estimate.

Lori-Ann said when the contracts are let the cost will be set in concrete and there will be no room for further negotiations. I have a certain amount of money to spend no more no less. She signed up entertainers from Hollywood, Los Vegas, and Paris, France. Food caterers of national recognition were assigned a part of the action. She featured a hot air balloon ride, a helicopter tour of the city, and a volunteer boxing match using party participants.

Scheduled was a women's topless mud wrestling match all party participants welcome. There were three large food-serving buffets on the outside terrace along with a set down dinner eating cove inside. Miss Lori-Ann scheduled three dance bands. Two will be playing at the same time. One inside and one on the GREY HOUSE DC terrace. The three bands will rotate from outside, inside and rest. When the plan was all put together, Miss Lori-Ann presented it to The President. The President asked a few questions to make sure all bases were covered. Finally, the President said, "Good job Miss Lori-Ann I could not have done better myself. Now we need to get this thing scheduled and published. We need to send out invitations by mail at least one month before the event takes place. Make certain that all major contributors receive an invitation. Please coordinate this with Thomas Vincent Zachariah."

After more planning and adjusting of the schedule, a date was set for the big event. The gala event started promptly at 7:00 PM.

Two big bands were banging up a storm. Three wet bars were set up on the GREY HOUSE DC outside terrace and two wet bars served the guests inside. The booze was flowing like water down a river. Registered lobbyist Hammon Bacon was there with four of his loveliest blonds. Hammond brought along a new beauty this time. She was gorgeous in the face and was 5 feet 7 inches tall but weighed only 120 pounds. She was a little on the thin side. Claude Hammer the freelance lobbyist was there with one of his girlfriends. Dee Dee and Kan Kan Bowman, the two lesbian sisters, were there. Bulla Klinginghouse, the rich contributor, Tom and Linda

Epstein, Gilbert Isenheardt, the gay Senator, were there just to mention a few. Overall, there must have been 450 people at the Victory Celebration. People were eating, dancing and drinking like this would be the last party on earth. Hammon Bacon called his four lovelies aside and cautioned them about drinking too much. He said, "You must drink with the customers to be friendly but you actually pour the drink out when no one is looking. Hammon's new girl did not know the routine very well and she consumed way too much alcohol. She was a good dancer and the guys liked to dance with her. Hammond's new girl picked out one of the oldest Senators at the dance. She immediately began to talk about the immigration problem. The Senator said, "I don't give a damn about immigration, honey. All I want to do is to dance and hold you close, real close." The blonde-haired person said, "Oh, Senator." As she scratched his head, the hair top piece started to move. She grabbed the hair top piece and Said, "You don't need this." She pushed the top piece down into her Bra. She said, "I'll keep it nice and warm for you." After the dance number was over they sat down and she began talking again about the illegal immigration. The senator said, "Let's change the subject, Honey. I want to hear something about you." She said, "What you want to know, my dress size, my brassier size, the color of my panties, what is it you want to know?" The Senator said, "Just tell me anything you want me to know." She said, "can I tell you something and you not get mad?' The Senator said, "Sure, honey, you can tell me anything." She said, let's go to a motel." The Senator said, "No, honey. I would rather stay here with the music."

She said, "Don't you like me? Wouldn't you like to go to bed with me?" The Senator Said, "No, I wouldn't. You are too damn skinny and your tits are too small. Now give me my hair top piece and go find yourself another sucker." The blonde-haired person managed to stand up all right but when she made a sharp 90 degree turn to the left she lost her balance and fell flat on her face. Several men tried to pick her up but she said, "Take your hands off of me" to each one. She was unable to gain the upright position by herself and she would not accept any help. One of the Senators called 911 and she was taken to the emergency hospital. As she was going out the door on a gurney, Hammon Bacon came upon the scene. He told the blond to sleep it off and not to come back to the party. Hammon Bacon immediately pulled out his cell phone and called another one of his blond beauties. Hammon said, "Honey, I know that this is very short notice, but I am in a jam. My new girl, you know the thin one, had too much to drink and she fell. They took her to the emergency hospital. I need a girl to work the immigration deal. If you can do this for me, I will give you an extra hundred. These people are connected to the drug cartel and if I do not do a good job for them, they may send a hit man after me." He could be heard to say, "Oh, come on, you don't have anything to wear. Honey, you would look good in a paper sack. Look, if you can get here in the next 30 to 45 minutes, I will make it an extra grand. I knew you would see it my way. See ya Hun."

The replacement blond arrived at THE GREY HOUSE DC exactly 40 minutes after Hammon hung up his phone.

She was a living doll. Hammon greeted her and gave her the instructions for the pitch on the immigration deal. By now, the party was in full swing. It seems like everyone had his or her fair share of liquor. The laughter was loud the music was even louder. People were dancing in the hallway and out on the grass. There was a little hugging and kissing in some of the out of the way places in THE GREY HOUSE DC. Everyone had a drink in hand. Occasionally someone in would get up to the microphone and try to make a speech. However, they were quickly drowned out by boos and laughter. Another dance partner approached that same Senator that was dancing with the skinny drunk blonde-haired person. She said, "Hi, buster want to dance with a lady with a full chest?" The Senator said, "Sure, why not." The woman must have weighted at least 250 pounds. She stepped on the Senator's toes a dozen times during one dance number. The Lady said, "It sure is a pleasure for me to dance with a real live Senator. You know you are my type. I could just hug you to death. Do you like to be hugged, Senator? I am a good hugger. I like to kiss too. Are you the kissing kind?" The Senator could smell the stale beer on her breath. Her mouth was wet with slobber.

She said, "Do you like girls with large breasts?" The Senator gently pushed her away and said, "No, I don't want to hug, or kiss and you are too damn fat for me. My poor toes are aching from being stepped on by your number eleven's. I just cannot take it anymore. Have a nice night" The Senator walked off the dance floor and left fatso standing there on the dance floor. The Senator found an unoccupied table. He took a seat and remover his shoes. He was drinking a martini on the rocks and when he thought no one was looking he poured the cold martini on his aching feet. Gilbert Isenheardt, the gay Senator from the mid-west, spotted the old Senator at the table obviously in distress. Gilbert seated himself at the old Senator's table and volunteered, "I bet you would like a nice foot rub." The old Senator replied, "Yes, I could sure use one." Gilbert said, "Well if you do not mind my scratchy hands, I think I could fix you right up, Senator. If you would like to come out to my van, I have some sweet smelling lotions that I think you would like. My van has the rear windows heavily tinted so no one can see us. We could have a little fun." The old Senator said, "I tell you what Senator, You take your sweet smelling lotion and stick it up your you-know-where. I am not about to let you touch my feet." Gilbert left in a huff. It was not long after Gilbert left the old Senator that Miss Karen Berkowitz, Secretary of defense, sat down at the old Senator's table. She said, "Well Senator is you having a good time? You must have as I see you have your shoes unattached. Too much dancing I presume?" The old Senator replied, "Yes, I am having a ball, Karen. First, a drunken skinny woman propositioned me. Then a big fat girl wanted me to go to bed with her. Finally, a gay Senator wanted to rub my feet.

Now what more could you ask for at a victory celebration party?" Karen said, "If you put your shoes back on, I'll dance with you, and I promise not to proposition you." The old

Senator said, "That's a deal, Karen." Karen and the old Senator danced two numbers. Karen had on a very low front cut evening dress. She had on a brassier that was about two sizes too small. The old Senator kept glancing at her breast. During the second dance, the occasional glance turned into a constant stair. Karen said to the old Senator, "Now look up into my eyes, Senator," then she gave out one big laugh. After the second dance with the old Senator, Karen said, well I guess I better leave you alone, I don't think you can take much more, Senator." Karen spotted the young Congressman, Daniel Bachelor, and said, "Good night" to the old Senator as the two of them danced away. The old Senator continued to sit alone at his table. Two different servers supplied him with fresh martinis on the rocks. Five dance numbers passes and one band change before Karen returned to the old Senator's table. Karen was out of breath as she spoke, "You want believe this, Senator. I was just propositions by one of the two gay Bowman sisters. Kan Kan wanted to go to her car, hug, and kiss a little. I no more than shook her off and the other sister; Dee Dee wanted to do a threesome in her car. I think we had better stay together for mutual protection. However, you better put your eye balls back in your head." Another big uncontrolled laugh emerged from Karen.

On the outside terrace, a big dance was in progress. The temporary dance floor was crowded and many were dancing on the grass. Congressman Tom Epstein and his wife Linda Epstein were among the grass dancers.

As the booze began to take effect, it soon became the custom to tap the men partner on the shoulder and swap partners. Congressman Daniel Bachelor was dancing with one of Hammond's blonds when they accidentally bumped into Tom and Linda. Daniel immediately tapped Tom on the shoulder and they swapped partners. Tom was now dancing with the blond and Daniel was dancing with Linda. Linda had on the same kind of Evening dress as Karen Berkowitz. Her brassier was also two sizes too small and lots of flesh was showing. Daniel commented on how lovely she looked in that evening dress. He said, "I really like the top part of your dress it really makes things stand out" Linda said, "Daniel behaves yourself" Linda said, "Daniel, you shouldn't talk like that." At this point Daniel held Linda very close as they danced. All at once, Daniel felt a gentle tap, tap on his shoulder. It was Tom, and they changed partners again. Tom and Linda would dance one number and sit out the next one. They would dance one and rest one. During each rest period, Linda would consume a large part of a strawberry Daiquiri. Daniel danced with several young girls and it was over an hour before he could get back with Linda. He saw Linda with another partner not Tom. He danced his way over to her and tapped the man on the shoulder. Daniel asked Linda if she was mad at him. She said, "Why should I be mad at you?"

"You see that man over there," Daniel, pointed to a drunk leaning against the open doorway to the inside dance floor. I just paid him twenty-five dollars to turn the lights out for 30 seconds in the middle of the next dance." Linda said, "Daniel, you didn't" "Yes I did Linda," said Daniel. Linda said, "I'm going to tell Tom." Daniel said, "Ok, I was just joking." Linda and Daniel did not dance together any more that night.

One of Hammon Bacon's beautiful blonds saw Congressman Paul Nelson alone at the wet bar. She asked the Congressman if he was having fun at the party. The Congressman answered, "You bet I am. But the music is way too loud." The Blond said, "Why don't we go outside and dance on the grass. The band out there is not nearly as loud as in here." Paul Nelson said, "That sounds like deal." He took the blonde-haired person by the arm and walked outside. As they passed the band Paul commented, "This band is as loud as the one inside." The blond said, "We can dance on the far end of the terrace and it won't be so loud."

As they danced, the blond asked the Congressman, "Do you think it is right to send an illegal immigrant back and leave their baby here. The baby is an American citizen if born here, you know. It just doesn't seem right to bust up a family." Paul said, "It is a sad thing to separate any family?" The blonde-haired person said, "You know, we could legalize the parents and all three could stay together as a family. Paul said, "That makes since." The blonde-haired person said, "I knew you would see it my way. Hey, Paul you see that little shack right here. It is a maintenance storage building for the grounds keeper. It is unlocked. You want to take a look inside?" Paul said, "Sure." As soon as they stepped inside the blond threw her arms around Paul and gave him, a big wet passionate kiss. The blond said, "You are going to vote 'yes' on the house bill HB 1190KP aren't you" Before Paul could answer the blond placed another passionate kiss on his lips. Paul said, "I'll make a note of it." The blond asked Paul "is there was anything else you would like to do here in the shack? I'm all yours, honey." Paul said, "There is no lock on the door and if we were caught it would ruin his career. So no thanks. Let's get back to the dance." Once outside the little shack the blond took off to look for another customer. One of Hammon's older blonds gave her usual pitch to Congressman Kent Miller. She was trying to get the drinking age lowered so the liquor industry could sell more liquor. She also applied pressure on Congressman Steven Boyd. Her main theme with Congressman Boyd was the prevention of some teenage pregnancies. The other older blonde-haired person in Hammon's organization was promoting the elimination of the concealed weapons law. She danced with Congressman Norman Christopher and Congressman Greg Biggs most of the night. She was pretty well convinced that she had their votes as she rubbed her highly perfumed body all over both of them. Bulla Klinginghouse, old money bags, danced almost every dance. She reminded each of her partners of her important contributions that made the victory celebration possible. Claude Hammer, the freelance lobbyist, did not dance with anyone else except his wife.

She had on a very expensive one of a kind black evening dress, which came, all the way up to her neck in the front.

There was no exposed skin in the front. There were two thin straps on each side of her neck that crossed over in the back. The back was open from her neck all the way to her butt. You could not help but get a hand full of flesh while dancing with her. She danced with several Congressmen and gave each one the pitch that her husband taught her. Eileen Barlow, the GREY HOUSE DC Press Secretary came over and sat down at Lori-Ann Carlson's table for a little friendly chat. Eileen asked, "how do you think the party went?' Lori-Ann said, "Oh, It went great. We met all of our goals. Seven of the guests had to be transported to emergency, not counting Hammon's skinny blond; so far, twenty-six couples had designated drivers take them home, The GREY HOUSE DC taxi charter service just loaded the one hundred and fifth couple for a safe trip home. The party is pretty well thinned out now."

The President is going to make a speech in a few minutes. Look there he is now." The president began to speak, "Well folks, it is 2:00 AM and the party is about over. I think you could say it was a great success by anybody's standard. No one got seriously hurt; there were many laughs. Lot of fun, lot of dancing, and the bands were great. I want to thank all of you for coming and I am looking forward to our next party here at THE GREY HOUSE DC. For the rest of you still here, drive carefully. I will need you for work first thing Monday morning. One final word, "I want to thank Miss Lori-Ann Carlson for putting together such a wonderful party. Thank You."

The President's Wooden Stool

The President uses a swivel chair on rollers behind a highly polished walnut desk. Just over his left shoulder is a four-legged wooden stool. Originally, it was too high but the Grey House DC carpenters cut the legs off to suit the President. The seat on the stool comes up to the Presidents chin.

The President has chosen some very attractive young women for his office staff. He has arranged for the news media to assign only reporters that meets his approval. All are very young and attractive women.

The Presidents executive desk comes equipped with a remote control door-locking device. One of the criteria for choosing office staff and female reporters is to have them set on the wooden stool.

The office staff and reporters would compare notes when a new girl came out of the President's office. The President would then make an entry into his private diary.

REPORTER LYNETTE DOUCH
FIRST VISIT

Thomas Vincent Zachariah has been the President's Personal Secretary Ever since the President took office. Thomas is six feet three inches tall and weighs 250 pounds. He is strictly all business, a no bull shit kind of person. You just do not argue with Tom.

All of the Presidents Visitors must be cleared through Thomas Vincent Zachariah, the President's personal secretary. Tom would then give a formal introduction of the visitor to the President. "Mister President may I introduce Miss Lynnette Douch of the KCNNP news agency. She is here for a scheduled exclusive Presidential interview for her magazine." The President responded, "Thank you Tom, you may be excused and close the door behind you." "Well how is your day Miss Douch? Do they call you Lynn or Lynnette?" asked the resident. "Lynn is fine Mr. President and thank you for asking. I want to thank you for granting me this Exclusive interview." The President said, "You are most welcome. Now what can I do for you?" She said, "The magazine would like to know what your busy day is like. What chores do you personally handle by yourself?"

The President responded, "Well we start the morning off with a military briefing. What is the status of our strike force? Are we up to the required strength? Then we have a," What If" session this is followed by any recommendations that the arm force chiefs may care to make. Then we have a budget conformance statement by the secretary of the treasury. How about some budget cuts? Can we raise taxes? Then I have presentations of world events. What is Russia doing? What is China Doing?" How is the unrest in the Middle East going? Are the nuclear arms talks on track? How about Iran and North Korea? Then we have the political considerations. What do the people want? Well as you know I have to sign off on every bill that congress passes. One of the things that I have been seeing is that trying to fit everything into your daily schedule is a challenge. In addition, I must keep abreast of the bills in the house and in the Senate so I can advise the legislators of my thinking. Lynn, there is no way that I can keep up with all of the stuff that congress comes up with. I have a staff that does a summary of each bill and the cabinet reviews this and a second summary of the summary are developed along with recommendations. This summary of the original summary can only be one page long with a maximum of 250 words. I do not even read the summary. My secretary reads it to me. Then I have presentations of world Economics, Global-warming World banking situation. Then there is the current currency exchange rate. Are foreign governments buying too much of our treasury notes? What effect on our trade deficit will the impending rate of money exchange have? Can we control the rate of exchange? Is the bank closures rate going up or going down? How about the home foreclosure rate? Do we need Immigration reform? Is the Federal Reserve holding the line on inflation or can we ease up some? Then finally, we have people like you, the news reporters. Lynn, put your pencil down and let us talk on a personal basis. Reporters are seeking an exclusive interview with the president like crazy. At the news conferences, the reporters fight over a chance to be heard. What I need is a news media coordinator to schedule and screen the reporters so that my time is used more efficiently. How would like to have that job at $ 60,000 per year? Lynn said, "I would love to have that job, but I am not sure I am qualified."

The President said, "Well we will have to see about that." Lynn changed the subject a bit by asking, "By the way Mr. President there are rumors in the pressroom about your wooden stool. Would you explain? Sure, said the President, "but keep this between you and me. Would you like to try the wooden stool out? "I was hoping that you would ask," responded Lynn. The President said, "Ok, Come around here and set on the stool. This is a sample of the way I like to do an interview." The President said. "I am sorry miss Douch but I am going to have to have to break this meeting off as I have a staff meeting in five minutes to discuss the GREY HOUSE DC stands on the federal legalization of medical marijuana," Said the President as he concluded the meeting.

SUSAN MEYER-REPORTER

Tom the President's personnel secretary made his usual introductory speech, "Mr. President, may I introduce Miss Susan Meyer of the syndicated news. She is here on a scheduled five minute interview with the President." The President responded, "Thank you Tom, and close the door behind you." Susan began by saying, "Mr. President My name is Susan Meyer of the syndicated press as Tom said. The reason for my visit is that my magazine and the syndicated news were so pleased with the interview you gave Miss Lynnette Douch that they want to do a series of interviews. In fact, they have already given the series a name, "Chats with the Prez." We know that your time is very valuable. The purposed interviews would last only five minutes. Oh, may I set on the stool, please." The President responded, "Sure, Have a seat." Susan took her seat on the wooden stool and pulled her dress up well above her knees.

Susan did not have on any hose and she said, "How's this Mr. President?" The President looked at her bare knees and said, "Great Miss Meyer." Susan said, "The actual interview will take only 5 minutes. We will need about 3 minutes to set up the camera in addition, to do the makeup. It will take about 2 minutes to tear down and, get out of here. Therefore, the whole show should take only 10 minutes of your valuable time. My boss said that you could use your time on each interview to cover any political issue that you would like to get across to the public. He said that this would be a win-win situation for both of us. The President said, "Well I think your 5 minutes are up and I have a meeting on the Federal involvement in embryo research. Have a good day Miss Meyer."

REPORTER-LYNETTE-DOUCH
SECOND VISIT

It was exactly one month after reporter Lynette Douch interviewed the President that she returned to The Grey House DC. Lynette secured a second visit to the President's office. Tom made his usual introduction speech when he introduced Lynnette Douch to the President for the second time. He told the President that this was scheduled follow-up visit from an earlier interview. Miss Douch said, "I want to thank you again Mr. President for giving me time from your busy schedule. As you know, my boss and the Magazine loved my write-up from our last visit. They liked it so much that they are going to do a series based upon our last interview." The President said, "Yes, so I have heard." My boss did not think I was qualified to do the series so he gave the job to Miss Susan Meyer." The President said, "Yes, I know, I interviewed Miss Meyer last week." Lynnette asked, "The last time I was here you said something about a new job as media coordinator. Is that job still open and do you think I qualify? I would do most anything to get that job." The president said, "Well the job has not been posted, in fact we don't even have a job description. The job qualification and requirements have not been written. Lynnette said, "I sure would like to have that job, Mr. President. By the way, do you ever set on the wooden stool? You know kike I did. "The President responded, "Yes, A few times." Miss Lynnette Douch said, "would you like to set on it for me?"

The President said, "Miss Lynnette Douch I think you qualify just fine. What you need to do in the next few days is to write-up a list of job qualification requirements and a job description. At this point the President presses"07" on his desk communicator machine. Tom came running in and said, "Yes, Mr. President I received your message on my pager." The President said, "Tom you remember the discussion we had on the need for a news media coordinator? Well Miss Lynnette would like to have that job and she seems to be qualified. I asked her to write up the job description and the required qualifications. I want you to put this information through the mill and get things rolling if you please." Tom replied, "Sure thing Mr. President." Tom turned towards Miss Lynnette Douch and said, "Well Miss Lynnette since you are going to write the job description and job qualification requirements, I'll bet you get the job. Will that be all Mr. President?" The President said, "Tom that will be all and close the door behind you." Lynnette I have a Cabinet meeting in a few. This room will be full of people in about two minutes so we have to conclude our meeting now. Thank you for coming in."

LAW ENFORCEMENT

Congressman Norman Christopher had to gobble his lunch down in a hurry. He was responsible for a major speech in the House of Representatives in 45 minutes. His companion for lunch today was Miss Susan Meyer a syndicated news reporter. Susan was the one that was to deliver the actual speech. It took 35 minutes by taxi from the Pennsylvania avenue government general cafeteria to the house auditorium. They had 10 minutes to spare. The mighty voice of the sergeant-at-arms rang out through the house auditorium, "Take your seats Ladies and Gentlemen, and please take your seats." BANG, BANG went the gavels as he announced, "The house is now in session, If you please Madam Speaker." The Speaker of the house made the following introduction, "Each member of the house of representatives will have 10 minutes to give their position on the matter before us today. At the end of the discussion there will be a roll call vote on HR-OK0039pp rev a. Let the discussions begin."

"Madam Speaker of The house, my name is Norman Christopher, Chairman of the House Law Enforcement Committee. I want to yield my 10 minutes to Miss Susan

Meyer Syndicated News Reporter. She will read in its entirety an article to be published in the, 'Grunts' magazine next month. I want this article to be recorded as a permanent part of the congressional record. If you please madam speaker." "You may precede Mr. Christopher." Answers the speaker of the house. Miss Susan Meyer began by thanking the members of the house for this opportunity to address the members of Congress.

"When we as a people decided to come out of our individual caves and climb down from the trees and live in communities it became apparent that we could take advantage of the skills that some members possessed. For example, Alex was good at sharpening stone axes while Redblood was an excellent hunter. Old Dogwood's wife made clothing and other items that required sewing. Sawbuck was good at gathering wood while his wife was a gourmet cook. It is a fact that Redblood would bring back more meat than a party of ten other hunters would. This happened consistently. Nobody could make axes and arrowheads like Alex. Therefore, you see living in a close net community has many advantages.

One-day two villagers got into a fight using Alex's stone axes because each one wanted the single piece of meat at the Redblood meat shop. On the way home, one of the fight participants ran over a little old woman on her bicycle. It soon became apparent that we needed some rules or laws to govern the behavior of the residents as they react with one another. However, who is going to make these rules or laws? Well now, let us see. We have Redblood as a hunter because he is good at it. Alex is the village axes man because he is good at his trade. We need to find some people that would be good at making laws. One of the residents went around and asked each resident if they would be interested in the position of lawmaker. He wrote the names down on a stone tablet of the residents that said they would like to be a lawmaker. He then called a meeting of the residents under the big oak tree. He read the names off the stone tablet.

He said, "raise your hand up for the candidate of your choose as I read their names. We are going to call this silly action, "VOTING". Well, anyway we now have a panel of three lawmakers.

Now I live on the east end of an east-west boulevard. There is not much traffic on "RED" boulevard. I am the only person living on this street. Right in the center of town RED boulevard crosses another highway called, "HOT" Avenue.

Now one of the first laws that the new law-making panel passed was to put "STOP SIGNS" on each corner of the RED—HOT intersection. They also placed 35 MPH maximum speed limit signs on each highway one quarter of a mile from the intersection. Now I have a red convertible mustang GT that likes to go 80 mph. I really hate to go 35 mph when the car wants to go 80 mph. I do not like the stop sign either. Therefore, I just do not stop at the intersection and cruise on through at 80 mph. Two weeks ago a resident moved into an apartment on the south end of HOT Avenue.

This person works at a factory on the north end of HOT Avenue. He has a Ferrari 250 GTO. His car will do 100 mph with ease. He, like me, does not like the stop signs at the RED-HOT highway intersection. He also hates to hold his 100 mph car to a measly 35 mph in the restricted speed zone. On his way to work, he buzzes through thru the RED-HOT intersection at 100 mph. The residents near the highway intersection wring their hands and say, "Oh My, They shouldn't do that."

At the next town meeting under the big oak tree, this situation was brought to the attention of the law-making panel. It looks like we need some sort of an enforcement mechanism. One of the residents suggested, "Why don't we tax each resident 25 polywigs (1,200 polywigs = 1 dollar USA) and hire a big guy to enforce the laws and pay him out of the treasury?" That same person that supervised the vote before stepped forward and the suggestion was put to a vote. He said, "The eyes have it. We will have a law enforcement officer and we will call him the, 'SHERIFF.' Well it was not long before the new sheriff arrested my neighbor for driving his Ferrari 110 miles per hour in a 35 mph max speed zone in addition, failing to stop at a stop sign. There was no jail in the community to house this dangerous criminal. The sheriff did find a log chain and a pad lock. The sheriff changed the criminal to the big oak tree where we had our town meetings. It was hot and the sheriff figures that his new criminal should have some water. He washed out, "CHARLIE'S" water bowl, filled it with water, and gave it to his criminal. The person looked hungry but the only thing in the house was a leftover can of, "ALPO." Charlie liked Alpo before he died so, it must be good. The sheriff opened the can of Alpo, put the contents into a nice clean dish, and presented it to the chained up criminal. The sheriff was sure that Charlie would not mind the criminal eating his Alpo and drinking out of his water bowl. The next morning two old women discovered the criminal chained to the big oak tree. They summoned two more women and they had a mini-meeting under the big oak tree. One woman said, "This is no way to treat one of our citizens." Another woman spoke up and said, "He didn't even have a chance to defend himself." "Yes," said another woman it looks like a clear case of police brutality." The fourth woman said, "His civil rights were violated." Another woman responded, "If you look close enough you can see some racial profiling." Another woman said, "yes, and discrimination too. We need to make some new laws." Another woman said, "Yes, and change some of our old laws."

The first lady said, "We are going to call an emergency meeting and get this thing resolved." The four old women went door-to-door gathering support for their cause. They notified others of the impending town hall meeting under the big oak tree. Four hours later a town hall meeting was convened under the big old oak tree. The four old women presented their case for civil rights violation. It was granted that some rules of conduct were necessary to guarantee that each citizen's civil rights were protected. It was also decided to vote upon the release of the dangerous criminal from the chains that bound him to the big old oak tree. The sheriff spoke up and said, "If you release this dangerous criminal from the tree, what am I supposed to do with him. We need a jail house." One of the women spoke up and said, "Let's tax each resident based upon their personal property evaluation and build a jail house." The raised hand took the vote. Two people voted for the proposal and thirty-six voted against the proposal. Fifty-three citizens did not vote at all. There will be no personal property tax and there will be no jailhouse. One old woman was heard saying to another, "You know that jail house thing was voted down because of costs. I have an idea. Let us pitch a tent to house the dangerous criminal. We could get old Dogwood's wife to make an orange colored suit for the dangerous criminal. That way we can tell the criminal from the rest of us. The tent will be handy if the sheriff captures any more criminals. We can chain all the criminals together and make a chain gang. This should save a bunch of money. "We cannot leave the dangerous criminal chained to the big oak tree," said one of the little old women. It was then voted upon to set the dangerous criminal free to mingle in the community.

Someone spoke up and said, "We need a head guy to oversee the operation of our little village. A little old woman spoke up and said, "Let's call this guy the Mayor." Someone else spoke up and said, "There should be a super head guy to oversee all of the villages in the land. A second little old woman spoke up and said, "Let's call this guy the 'President.'" Another person spoke up and said, YES, and there should be a branch of government that makes the laws for all of the land. A third person spoke up and said, "great let's call the bunch of people that makes the laws,' Congress' and the super head guy, 'President'." Some one behind the big old oak tree said, "Shouldn't we spell out the duties of this super head guy we are going to call President?" Another person also behind the big old oak tree said, "Let's put him in charge of securing our borders."

At the next meeting under the big old oak tree, one of the members spoke up and said, "You know, we ought to have some kind of a head guy to keep all of the Mayors in line." A little old lady joined in and said, "Yes, and lets call this head guy 'Governor'." That same member said, "You know old Sneekingfelter is a good actor I bet he would make a wonderful Governor. Another member added, "I saw him in the movie 'Super Guy' he took on twelve armed men single handed." Another member spoke up and said, "And he had one hand tied behind his back." The first to speak on this subject said, "Let's talk to old Sneekingfelter and see if he will take the job." A third member added, "I went to acting school and took a correspondence course on the internet, I think I could handle the job of super head guy we call President." The member acting as the moderator of the meeting announced, "OK, we will put your name on the ballot for next November's election. The monitor asked, "What qualifications do you have to be Mayor Mister Burgenjerk?" Mr. Burgenjerk answered, "Well I am as crooked as a rattle snake." "Good replied the meeting monitor. You are qualified to run as our next Mayor." Mr. Sneekingfelter asked Mr. Burgenjerk, "Just what do you intend to do if you are elected Mayor of our little Village?" Mr. Burgenjerk replied, "The first thing I will do is to put on a TV talk show with five of our best known women." Mr. Sneekingfelter asked, "What is going to be the theme of your TV talk show?" Mr. Burgenjerk replied, "Well it's hard to tell. You see all five women will be talking at the same time. No one will be listening. The show will be thirty minutes long and each woman will talk for the entire thirty minutes." Raging Cajon commented, "Man that sounds like a hit show already it should be very interesting." When asked about the name of the show, Mr. Burgenjerk replied, "I'm thinking about calling it 'The Vision'." Mr. Burgenjerk asked, "Mr. Sneekingfelter, just what are you going to do if you are elected Governor in November?" Mr.Sneekingfelter replied, "First thing I am going to learn how to smoke. Then I am going to buy a great big box of them fancy Cuban cigars. I am going to prop my feet up on top of my desk and look important. I will try real hard not to make anyone mad at me." Let us see we have on the ballot Mr. Sneekingfelter for Governor, Mr. Burgenjerk for Mayor, and Raging Cajon for super head person we call President.

The meeting monitor said, "Sounds like a plan to me" The Meeting Monitor announced, "Let's call it a day. It is getting hot here under the big old oak tree. The meeting is adjourned."

As the community grew bigger and bigger it was necessary to bring in some outside labor to help the farmers produce enough food to support the community. The cost of food for each resident's household was a significant part of their total income. The farmers were forced to look for the cheapest labor they could find. Many farmers hired workers that came from a foreign country. These foreign workers were happy as they were receiving more money on the farm in this country than they could get at home. The farmers were happy as the cost of labor using the foreign workers were far less than using local workers were. Some of the local merchants and manufacturing businesses were unhappy with the influx of these foreign workers, as their businesses were not benefiting from their presence. Some of the local laborers also complained because the foreign workers were taking their jobs away. A town hall meeting was called to discuss this situation. Both parties brought the pros and cons to light. It was pointed out that if the foreign workers were not allowed to work in the fields a head of lettuce would eventually cost five dollars apiece. Tomatoes would be one dollar each. The cost of food for each household would take 80% of the total household income. This would wreck our economy in short order. One of the little old women spoke up and said, "What we need is some laws to regulate the number of foreign workers allowed into our country. That way we can have cheap food and our workers won't lose their jobs." This action was put into a motion and put to a vote. The resolution was passes unanimously. We now have laws that regulate the number of foreign workers allowed into our country each year. Someone spoke up and said, "Who is going to enforce the new laws we just passed." A mysterious voice was heard to say, "Let's give this job to our new super head guy that we now call the President?" As the foreign workers attempted to cross the border at the regular crossings, many were turned back because the quota had been filled. These workers found many crossing points that were not staffed by border patrol officers. They would cross over to their old jobs and continue to work and collect their money as usual. The local communities asked the federal government for help. The Congressional representatives from each district along with the Senators pass some laws similar to the local statutes.

Much like our sheriff without a jail or other means of law enforcement, the federal government had found that enforcing the immigration laws too hot to handle. Politics is the name of the game. If it were politically expedient to enforce any law, it would be enforced. If it is not politically expedient to enforce a particular law just let it lay it may just go away.

I used to feel guilty as I speed through the 35 MPH speed zone and past the STOP SIGNS at 80 MPH. However, I do not feel that way anymore. If the Executive branch of the

Federal Government can pick-and-choose, the laws that they want to obey and enforce, then why can't I?

Now our poor sheriff tries to enforce the immigration laws the federal government refuses to address. From all the criticism he receives you would think that the sheriff was the criminal that needed to be chained to the big old oak tree.

Our dangerous criminal was setting under the big old oak tree with a very dry martini in his left hand and a half eaten Macintosh apple in his right hand listening to the proceedings. He could not hold back his laughter any longer, so he spoke, "Tell you what folks, I will hold my speed down to the speed limit and even stop at the stop signs at the intersection just as soon as your super head guy you call the President enforces the immigration laws and secures our borders.

All three of our candidates were successful in the November election. That maybe because they were unopposed. No one else wanted the jobs. We now have Burgenjerk as the Mayor of our little hamlet. Sneekingfelter is our new Governor. The super head guy we call President is now Raging Cajon. It was not long after the election when Redblood spotted three foreign hikers on our side of the border. He reported his findings to the Sheriff. The Sheriff promptly arrested the three hikers and charged them with espionage. The sheriff brought the three hikers to the big old oak tree for a hearing. A quick meeting was convened under the tree. The sheriff said that the three hikers were charged with espionage. A little old woman spoke up and said, "Why would anyone want to spy on our little hamlet? There is nothing here but us folks." The sheriff said, "The three hikers were dangerously close to our secret underground nuclear facility." The woman said, "I did not know that we had a secrete underground nuclear facility?" The sheriff responded, "Oh, yes we have three of them." The little old woman asked, "Sheriff, what are you going to do with the three hikers?" The sheriff responded, "I am going to let one go free and put the other two on the chain gang for eight years. They can sleep in 'tent city' at night."

LITTLE JOSEPH

Lobbyist Hammon Bacon was having supper at the motel restaurant when his cell phone rang. It was that foreign gang with the drug cartel money. The wanted some action on their request to have a law passed that would legalize the migrant parents of a child born in the USA. They were not very polite. They said, "If it takes more money, just speak-up." Hammon Bacon said, "Let me talk to one of my Congressman, and we will try to have a bill on the floor by the middle of next week. That is as soon as I can make it. With this kind of a rush, it will take another 12 grand." They said, "The money will be in your account tomorrow. Now let us see some action on your part. Got it?" Click. The phone went dead.

Hammon Bacon called Congressman-Norman Christopher and Told him of the phone call he just received. Hammon Bacon said, "These guys mean business. Look can you slop together a bill real quick and present it on the floor and do a dog and pony show with one of the system victims?" Let us see if we can conclude this thing! Oh, yes I have another twelve grand for expenses." The congressional representative said, "Well it will take another ten grand for my expenses."

Hammon Bacon said, "Let's move at lightning speed. I'm afraid of these guys." Congressman Norman Christopher brought in three extra contracts writers and the bill was ready in three days. A phone call and a lunch later with the speaker of the house the bill was scheduled for debate the following Monday morning. This swift action cost Hammon another cool five grand of cartel money.

As soon as the house of representatives was brought to order the speaker of the house said, "We are now open for discussion on HB 11181-KT. It has to do with the legalization of migrant parents of off springs born in our country. We will go down the list by seniority and each congressional representative will have ten minutes for debate. Two of the congressional representative before Norman yielded their ten minutes to congressional representative Norman. When it came Norman's time to speak, he had thirty minutes to make his presentation. Congressional representative Norman stood before the assembly, thanked the speaker of the house, the Ladies and Gentlemen of the congress and said, "I would like for all of you to meet little Joseph. Say hi Joseph. Six years ago Joseph's father, Manuel Rodriguez snuck across our border with two other foreigners at night. Each one had two 16 ounces bottles of water in their back pockets. They each had a pork chorizo sandwich wrapped in a flour tortilla in their side pockets. It was dark at night as they made their way through prickly pear cactus, saguaro cactus, choya cactus, ocotillo cactus and verdi cactus. There were sidewinder rattlesnakes and scorpions in the desert at night. The three was lost and wondered through the desert in a senseless faction. Three days later, two of the three made it to a small American village on the border. Exhausted, hungry, and thirsty the two surviving men begged for food and water. A rattlesnake bit the third men and his leg swollen up so bad he could not walk. He was left in the desert to die. Manuel Rodriguez was one of the Survivors. The people that took Manuel Rodriguez in said they knew of a farm that needed some farm labor. They also knew of a house where many workers lived. Manuel paid a visit to the recommended house.

It was a three-bed room house with two bathrooms. Each bedroom has two beds in it. There are four beds in the living room. The ten beds would sleep 20 people. The property owner said he did not have room for Manuel now but he could place an old army cot in one of the bedroom closets. The property owner said he would not charge Manuel for sleeping in the closet on the cot. Manuel said that was great because he did not have any money anyway. The property owner told Manuel he could sleep on the cot until he could find room for him on a regular bed. One of the bedrooms provided sleeping quarters for two married couples. The rent on the three-bed room house was $1,000.00 per month. This divided among the 20 residents amounted to $ 50.00 per month each.

Most of the residents in the house worked on a large four hundred acre onion farm. Manuel had no trouble being hired to pull green onions. The onion farm provided three meals a day with each meal break only 10 minutes long. He worked from 6:00 AM to 8:00PM at night. He earned $5.00 per hour or $ 70.00 per day. Out of these seventy dollars per day, he was able to send $ 300.00 per month back home to support his wife and her mother. In six months' time, he saved up $10,000.00. He sent $8,000 back home to pay some human smugglers to bring his wife across the border. These were drug smuggling people with lots of experience crossing the border. Manuel and his wife were able to get one of the beds in the house that was reserve for married couples.

It was not long before Manuel's wife became pregnant with little Joseph. Joseph was born in the USA. He is a citizen of the USA. His parents are undocumented residents.

The current law states that undocumented residents must be deported to their original country. We have three alternatives. One we can send the parents of little Joseph back across the border and let little Joseph become a ward of the stare. Two: we could send all three back across the border, but whoa Joseph is a citizen of the USA you cannot treat a citizen that way. Joseph has all of the rights that our constitution and its amendments allow. Little Joseph is not a criminal. Why should we send him to a foreign country that he has never seen before? This would be punishment for a crime he did not commit.

Three: we could legalize little Joseph's undocumented parents and all three could live here as three have done for the last three years. Members of Congress, Manuel has never been arrested, he has never had a traffic ticket; he does not even have a car.

He attends church each Sunday. He has to make up his Church attending time by additional work in the onion fields. He has never caused any of his neighbors any trouble. He is not a criminal he is just undocumented. Look at this little boy does he look like a criminal? Now, Ladies and Gentlemen I ask you what is the right thing to do. Please vote yes on HB11181-KT. Thank you madam speaker for allowing me the time to present this horrible injustice in our laws. Thank you madam speaker. The speaker of the house called upon congressional representative Baker for the next debate.

Congressman Baker thanked the speaker of the house and then asked, "Can I just ask Congressman Norman Christopher one question before I start madam speaker? Congressman what do you do when a foreign woman that is 8 months pregnant sneaks across the border and has her off spring on American soil. This woman has not contributed to our economy. She had no effect on the price we pay for lettuce, onions, watermelons, or cantaloupes. Yet we must supply medical attention to her and her off spring. We must educate her child. Another point I would like to make is that legal pregnant tourist women can inter the USA. Some of these women have their babies here in the USA. This practice is dubbed "birth tourism." The practice of granting automatic citizenship to children born in the U.S., a right laid out in the 14th Amendment is resulting in an exploitation of the Constitution. This is a big drain on our already weak economy. As you purpose since the child is automatically a citizen the parents should also become citizens. They can live happily at our expense."

Representative Norman Christopher responded, "Well congressman, our system of government provides three separated branches of government. The Legislative branch makes the laws. The Executive branch executes the laws that the congress makes. Then we have the Judicial branch, which interprets the laws that congress makes. It is the responsibility of the Executive branch to enforce the laws that we currently have on our books. To answer your question Congressman Baker, the pregnant woman should not be here in the first place. In addition, while we are on this subject, We must be very diligent in the wording of the laws we make as the judges must interpret these laws so that they can be applied within the bounds set by our constitution. Otherwise, we may find ourselves in a box similar to the one we are in right now.

When the vote was tallied only four votes were against HB 11181=KT. The drug cartel leader congratulated Hammon Bacon and said, "You did an excellent job. In addition, we want to give you a little bonus." He gave Norman an envelope that contained 200 one hundred dollar bills.

HOUSEKEEPER QUACKENBUSH

Knock, Knock, "May I come in Mr. President?" asked the housekeeper. The President responded, "you may enter." "Mr. President, My name is Camilla Quackenbush the new GREY HOUSE DC housekeeper. Would you like for me to tidy up the place a bit?" The President responded, "sure go right ahead but don't touch anything on my desk." The president said to Miss Quackenbush, "You know that I have a six place eating area to the right of the big conference table. It is through those green double doors. You may want to look in there and see if it needs any attention. To the left of the big conference table is a set of blue double doors. Behind those doors is a private rest area. There is a large couch, an easy chair, and a single twin bed. The bed is not large enough to get a good night's sleep, but I can take a nap in there when I have had a busy day. You may want to tidy that up some."

The president could not help from watching miss Quackenbush as she bent over to dust the furniture in the round presidential office. After cleaning the main office, Miss Quackenbush gave her attention to the private eating area. Having finished the eating area she proceeded to the private rest area. The President followed her into the rest area saying, "you may need some help. I would like to turn the mattress over." Miss Quackenbush said, "I think I can handle it ok." The President responded, "Two hands are sometimes better than one." Turning the single twin bed mattress over was a snap. The President suggested that they fold up the old sheets and replace them with freshly laundered sheets and he offered to help with the folding. Camilla took one of the long ends of the sheet and the President took the other end. They folded the sheet in half. As the President walked towards Camilla to grab her folded sheet end, his hands struck her on her breasts. The President explained, "Oh, I'm sorry."

The President was way behind on his work so he sat behind the highly polished walnut executive desk and began to shuffle some papers. Two days later Camilla was cleaning the circular office and when she came to the wooden stool, she asked the President if she should clean it. He President said, "Go ahead, but it shouldn't need much cleaning as I keep it pretty tidy myself." Camilla asked the President if he ever sat on the stool. The President responded, "Oh yes, but I much prefer the side rest area." Camilla said, "I have heard so much about the wooden stool that I think I would like to try it.

The President suddenly stopped. He said, "I am sorry to interrupt our session but I am late for a forum on the Federal Government's involvement with mental-health. He rushed over to the polished walnut desk and pulled out a little black book. He thumbed through several pages and made a quick entry in the book. He took his top coat from the rack and put it on as he went out the door. He left the little black book on the desktop in plain view.

After the President left for his forum meeting, Camilla picked up the little black book and began to read. The front part of the book had some names and telephone numbers written down in random faction About half way through the book there was a list of girl's names on the left hand side of the book. The names ran from the top to the bottom of the page. On the right hand side of the open book, there were columns marked off and the heading at the top of the right side of the open book listed comments about each girl. Under each column there were little check marks. Camilla noticed her name on the left hand side of the open book. The President had checked off her name under one of the columns. Camilla took the little black book over to the copy machine and made a copy of the open book pages.

After cleaning the circular office room Camilla went to the press conference room where she found three other girls with names in the President's little black book. Camilla announced, "Come here girls, have I got news," She explained about finding the President's personal black logbook. She proceeded to tell of the entries she found in the book. Each girl asked all at once, "Is my name in there?" Camilla answered, "Yes, and it tells what he thinks of you. Oh, My God was the general response from each girl. "Here let me see," one of the girls asked. "Yes, me too." said another trying to get a glance of the notation by their names, Camilla folded up the torn black book copies and said, "We'll talk about these later girls. Camilla returned to her cleaning chores and the other girls began to cry.

POLITICAL BRIEFING

Knock, Knock, "May I come in Mr. President?" Tom asked. The President said, "Come in." Tom opened the door partway stuck his head in and announced, "your political briefing is in 4 minutes, Mr. President. The President said, "come on in Tom. I want you to stay for the political briefing. I have invited a few more people. I am not happy with the way things are going and I am going to make some changes."

The President called the meeting to order and said, "Just in case you-all do not know each other; I will introduce you as we go around the table starting on my left. First, we have Mr. Thomas Vincent Zachariah, my personal Secretary. Next to Tom is Miss Eileen Barlow THE GREY HOUSE DC Press Secretary. Next it Eileen we have Miss Lynnette Douch, THE GREY HOUSE DC News Media Coordinator. At the far end of the table, we have Mr. Damon Wineseller, Political Advisor to the President. He will conduct the meeting today. To his left is the Senate Majority Leader and next to him is the Speaker of The House of Representatives. Mr. Wineseller it's all yours." Mr. Wineseller started by saying, "The latest results of the statistical poles are not in our favor. When asked do you approve of the way the administration is handling the offshore oil-drilling problem. A random sampling of the voters in one of our southern States shows:

Twenty-three percent approve,

Forty-six percent disapprove,

Thirty-one percent undecided,

With a statistical margin of error of 3% it is quite clear that the majority of the voters do not like the way the administration is handling the offshore oil-drilling situation.

I would like to point out that the same poll was conducted when national gasoline prices were running above $4.00 per gallon. The results of this random sampling does show some improvement Forty-one percent approve.

Forty-three percent disapprove

Sixteen percent undecided

Again, I want to point out that these figures do shift somewhat as the economic conditions change. A random sampling of the voters in one of our mid-Atlantic States indicates that the voters are not happy with our stance on the Nuclear arms negotiations:

Thirty-eight percent approve

Forty-nine percent disapprove

Thirteen percent undecided

A random sampling of the voters in the mid-west shows that the voters do not like what we are doing in the global warming area:

Thirty-eight percent approve

Forty-five percent disapprove

Seventeen percent undecided

With a Plus or minus 3% margin of error you can see the dissention is not strong. The poles are now showing an even split on the illegal immigration issue. The results of a random sampling of the voters in our border states show an equal member for and against the administration current actions. "The President interrupts, "Mr. Wineseller, I am sick and tired of hearing about those random numbers and random people. Tom have you ever met a random person?" Tom responds, "No sir, I have not." The President continues, "Well neither have I. What I want is the opinion of real voters not some imaginary group somewhere up there.

I want some grass roots results. I want to know what the real voters are thinking. I could care less about your random people. I was voted into office by real warm-blooded people not some imaginary group that you cannot even shake their hands. Mr. Wineseller I want you go get me some results from real people. Those, "Purple Hat Ladies that were so helpful in the election campaign would be a good place to start. How about those people that rallied at the party picnic? How about using the list of campaign contributors. How about the volunteers that placed all of those signs in people's front yard. Mr. Wineseller there is plenty of real people out there. You do not need to be messing around with those imaginary soles. Why don't you question some people that you can slap on the back and shake their hand some women that you can hug and kiss? I want you to go out there and get me some grass roots voter results. Is That clear Mr. Wineseller?" "Yes Sir that is quite clear, Mr. President" The President says, "If there are no more statements or comments we will adjourn until next week at this same time."

INFLUENCE-MRI

In news, briefing at the GREY HOUSE DC it was reported that six of our experienced Navy Seals had been lost while performing a highly classified combat mission. Admiral Lee Wong Pucker called an emergency staff meeting to evaluate the new information. Admiral Pucker assigned various tasks to his staff members and told them to report back in 24 hours with a full report with recommendations. Armed with 6 thousand pages of information admiral Pucker set up a dinner and briefing meeting with key members of Congress. The meeting was held in a secure conference room in the Hexagon.

Admiral Pucker started the meeting with the statement that six of our finest Navy Seals were killed while performing a highly classified combat mission. He further explained that the mission was to sink an aircraft carrier belonging to a hostile country. The Navy Seals were to swim under water for two miles and attach explosive charges to the aircraft carrier and swim back to the waiting camouflaged fishing vessel. The explosive charges were packaged in a magnetic metal container. The packages were to be attached the aircraft carrier's metal hull.

This kind of operation has been performed many times with success. If fact the same Navy Seals had just returned from a mission off the coast of Israeh. There they sank a freighter carrying small arms to the Palerianean military extremists. Something new has been added to the picture. A machine has been developed by one of our unfriendly countries that can detect changes in the magnetic resonance image of their vessel.

The detection device operates on the same principal as the medical Magnetic Resonance Image (MRI) machine. Our Intelligence has informed me that some of the parts used in their machine are the same parts used in the Universal Electric's MRI Model 9000-Rev-3T. When the Magnetic Resonance Image of the vessel changes an alarm is set off and defensive action is taken. That is what happened to our six Navy Seals.

The Navy does not plan to abandon the Navy Seal operated explosive program but we must find a way to attach the explosives without using magnetic attraction. It has been suggested that the attachment could be made using special sea water resistant glue. A quick test of all the known glues indicates they all are water soluble while in the uncured state. That means that the glue will dissolve in the seawater before it sets up and the explosive charges will fall off the target vessel.

I am requesting our specifications department to draft up a set of specs. that will meet our very demanding requirements. I am asking Congress to appropriate sufficient under cover funds to finance this project.

Senator Gilbert Isenheardt, Chairman of The Senate Armed Services Committee, Interrupted Admiral Lee Wong Pucker by asking, "Admiral Pucker I see you have a sex thousand page report in hand. Can you give us a more detailed description of Enemy's Magnetic detection device and how it is used, please?" Admiral Pucker responded, "Sure Senator, I have a very good description of the devise from our intelligence people. The parts sources for the machine were very helpful in piecing together a good scenario.

Ladies and Gentlemen bear with me and I will try to make it as simple as possible." Admiral Pucker continued, "Back in elementary school we were taught that like poles on two different magnets will repel each other while opposite poles on two different magnets will be attracted to each other. One other piece of basic information is that magnetic lines of force are continues, that is, there is no beginning and end to a magnetic line of force. A third piece of basic information is that magnetic lines of force tend to push away from each other.

The core piece of equipment in the enemy's magnetic detection device is a very long electro magnet. The center of this magnet is made of bars of very soft iron. The magnet runs from the stern to the bow of the ship. When Direct Current is applied to this very long magnet, magnetic lines of force leave the stern's South Pole and travel up towards the North Pole in the bow of the ship. As the magnetic field gets stronger and stronger the ship's outer metal skin becomes saturated. Magnetic lines of force seek a path outside the ship's metal skin through the salty seawater.

Remember we said earlier that magnetic lines of force tend to push away from each other. The magnetic lines of force running alongside the vessel in the seawater tend to balloon out. When a Navy Seal approached the vessel, carrying an explosive magnetic package these lines of force will reach out and go through the Seal's metal package rather than continue through the seawater.

A magnetic density detector on board measures the magnetic density perpendicular the surface of the vessel. An operator inside the vessel can see the magnetic image of his vessel on a computer screen. The magnetic image is not important but any change in the magnetic image is very important. A change in the magnetic image of the vessel triggers an alarm device.

Let us go back to that very long electromagnet, the copper wire windings on the magnet are in seven sections. While in the standby mode, a sequencer fires each of the magnet segments independently. The operator can adjust the frequency and duration of each segment's "on time." The operator can get a very detailed or high definition picture of the vessel's magnetic image. The operator will throw a switch to connect all of the long magnet's segments series to give a much more powerful magnetic field when a change in magnetic image is detected in the standby mode. Well I hope I did not lose anybody during this not—so—short dissertation

Many of the lobbyists in DC work very close with members of Congress. Often classified information is exchanged between the two of them. That is what happened in this case. Mr. Randy Pitts Lobbyist representing the Paint, Janitorial, and Hardware interest got all of this information. Mr. Pitts has a personal interest in one of the largest adhesive manufacturing plants on the east coast. It is rumored that he has over one million dollars in the company stock and his brother-in-law is the CEO.

When the adhesive manufacturer CEO received the information from lobbyist Pitts, he immediately set up a Development and Research unit in his plant. A Physicist with an Applications Engineer as his assistant headed the new department. The CEO ran this information by his financial department. The financial department said that considering cost of development and the limited amount of sales the new sea water resistant glue would have to sell for $850.00 per ounce just to break even. Lobbyist Pitts said that would be no problem.

Lobbyist Pitts worked very closely with the Research and Development department at the adhesive plant. As soon as he gained any information about the new secret product, he would pay a visit to the Specifications Department in the Hexagon. His pitch at the Hexagon was that the sea water resistant glue had some special and unusual elements and these must be included into the final specification sheet. MR Pitts was very persuasive and a very a fast talker. He would not leave the Hexagon until he sold his point of view.

In the meantime, our old friend Free Lance Lobbyist Mr. Claude Hammer obtained the information on the Navy's need for a sea water resistant glues. He had worked with a small adhesive manufacturer on the West Coast several years ago and they were working on water resistant glue then. It turns out that they had water resistant glue with a very short shelf life. This product had to be stored at 35 to 38 degrees Fahrenheit in order to survive the water solvent. Mr. Hammer asked if the product was ready for the market.

The answer was yes and no. If the product reaches a temperature greater than 38 degrees Fahrenheit for more than 3 minutes it will freeze up. The shelf life under any conditions is less than 30 days. Mr. Hammer said he would like to take a small sample of the glue to the Hexagon to get their reaction.

Mr. Hammer walked into an open meeting being conducted by Lobbyist Pitts at the Hexagon with a six-pack cooler containing a sample of the West Coast glue. After Mr. Pitts made his presentation, Claude Hammer Stepped to the podium and announced that the six pack cooler in his hand contained the long sought after water resistant glue. Admiral Lee Wong Pucker asked to see the specifications for the subject glue. After looking the specifications over for a few minutes Admiral Pucker asked Lobbyist Hammer how in the hell can we keep this stuff at 38 degrees Fahrenheit in a 68 degree ocean for 3 minutes? It takes over two hours to swim to the target vessel sometimes. Mr. Hammer responded, "Come on Admiral these are minor problems and surely they can be overcome." Lobbyist Randy Pitts spoke up and said," Mr. Hammer take your six pack cooler and stick it up you know where," Admiral Pucker adjured the meeting and left the podium.

The Hexagon Specification Department was very busy drafting a comprehensive specification for sea water resistant glue. Many of the clauses in the spec. were a result of suggestions from lobbyist Pitts. The specification contained many items that matched the current manufacturing process of the East Coast Adhesive Manufacturer.

Finally, the specification was approved by Admiral Lee Wong Pucker and his staff. The spec. along with an invitation to bid was sent out to all known adhesive manufacturer. All adhesive manufacturers that hoped to submit a successful bid must send a sample of their product to an approved independent testing lab. The Lab would in turn send a report to the Hexagon with the test results.

Two very small adhesive manufactures in the Mid-West submitted samples of their glue to the approval process. In both cases, the glue met all the requirements called out in the documentation. The estimated cost of the glues was $ 37.50 per ounce and $43.00 per ounce. When lobbyist Pitts heard of this development, he rushed over to the Hexagon and talked the specification department into adding an addendum to the specification requiring that the glue must contain at least one percent hexachlorochueslime. This new additive is supposed to destroy coral bacteria that can attack the sea water resistant glue before it cures properly. Mr. Randy Pitts produced some fake test results showing the effectiveness of hexachlorochueslime. His East Coast adhesive manufacturer holds the patent on this product. They will not license other manufacturers to market it. The hexachlorochueslime addendum took a lot of persuasion to get the addendum into the spec. Two trips to the Bahamas, fifteen expensive dinners, an ocean going cabin cruiser, and two mountain resort log cabins and the deal was done. This new requirement added to the Sea Water Resistant Glue specification disqualified all of the adhesive manufacturers except for the East Coast Adhesive manufacturer represented by lobbyist Randy Pitts.

After much testing in the Hexagon Chemical Laboratory, The contract to supply the Navy with Sea Water Resistant Glue was awarded to Lobbyist Randy Pitts's Client on the East Coast. It was designated as SWRG-01 and entered into the Navy materials inventory.

On the very first try using the new SWRG-01, the explosive attachment was successful. However, the Navy Seals were detected swimming away and the enemy was able to remove the explosive packages and disarm them.

Lobbyist Randy Pitts also represents the Hardware interest and was able to make some suggestions. Randy said," How about adding a spring like on a mouse trap?"

The armament application Engineers at the Hexagon added a spring loaded device to the backside of the explosive package very similar to an old fashion mousetrap spring. The Navy Seal is instructed to set the spring before attaching the explosive package to the target vessel.

On a trial run in one of the abandoned naval shipyards, another Navy Seal was lost due to an explosive mishap. The target vessel had been in mothballs for twenty years. There was a large build-up of algae and coral on the vessel hull. The SWRG-01 did not hold and the explosive package slid off the vessel hull. The spring-loaded device detonated the explosive package before the Navy Seal could reset the spring device.

Lobbyist Randy suggested one of his client's potent cleaners to remove the algae and coral from the target vessel before applying the SWRG-01.

Admiral Pucker was called back to the Senate Armed Services Committee for an update on the Navy Seal problem. The Admiral gave the committee all of the information he had in his position. He did make one additional comment, "The last time I was here you asked for some more technical information on the enemy's magnetic detection device. Our Intelligence people have come up with another piece of the story. It seems that when the device is in the "Stand-by mode" the magnetic field is increased many fold. The turbo-diesel electric generators aboard the vessel charge a bank of twelve-volt storage batteries. These twelve-volt batteries in turn charge a large number of capacitors. These capacitors are discharged through the very long magnet producing a tremendous magnetic pulse. The magnetic force field has been detected by our armed forces aircraft one half mile away from the vessel. It seems that they are experimenting on the device and making improvements all the time. Well that is all the information that I can give you at this time. If there are no more questions, I have to leave for a NATO conference in Geneveron. Thank you very much.

After the meeting, Congressional Representative Steven Boyd commented to Senator Gilbert Isenheardt, Better keep a close eye on that Lobbyist Randy Pitts. Last year he got himself into a swindle with a bunch from Chicako. They were trying to sell discounted half-off coupons for eye examinations. The prescription from the examination was good only with the purchase of a pair of no-lenses eyeglasses. Senator Isenheardt questioned Congressional Representative Steven Boyd, "How in the heck can a thing like that work?" Congressman Boyd said, "The sales pitch goes something like this. When light is reflected, off of the target the lines of light cross over as they pass through a hole. The lines of light continue on until they reach the retina in the eyeball. The size and shape of the hole is very critical. Here is where the eye examination prescription comes to play. I understand they sold over a million of the coupons then went out of business. Senator Isenheardt said he heard a similar story about this guy. He tried his hand in the used car business. He bought a thousand used cars that were water soaked in the Katrina flood. He then bought an existing upholstery shop. He refurbished the water soaked cars interior and painted the outside. He set up a fake used car dealership in the State of New York and sold the vehicles with no guarantee. Many of the cars had water in the motor crankcase and the transmission housing. Some of the cars even had water in the rear end differential unit. After a few months, these cars began to develop engine and transmission problems. They promptly closed up shop and moved to Floriga. Congressional representative Boyd said, "It's been rumored that he tried to sell seats on the shuttle for a trip to the moon. Senator Isenheardt said, "It's also rumored that he got with a group that tried to sell the ides of a gasoline automobile engine running on water.

INFLUENCE-Candy

Mr. Butter Payne better known as" Butt Pain" invited Senator Knott Hurd to be a guest on his national TV talk show. The subject to be discussed on this particular session of the show will be "The Evils of Outside influence on members of Congress."

The BUTTER PAYNE TV SHOW is always taped in advance of the actual airing in order to prevent any embarrassing moments being broadcast should they occur.

The interview started in the usual manor with Mr. Payne giving a prepared TV Station approved dissertation on the evils of the outside influence on Congress by lobbyist. TV talk show host then turns to face Senator Knott Hurd and comments, "Speaking of influence Senator Hurd let me tell you a story I know from first hand. During World War II, I was a news correspondent for a syndicated news agency. We were allowed to go up to the front lines with the troupes during enemy engagement. I was partnered with a young soldier from the state of New Jersey. He was bitter, dirty, tired, and hungry. I asked him if there was any little thing that Army could do to make his life a little more bearable under these combat situations. His answer was this, "You know we get up out of our sacks at 6:00 AM every morning. The first breakfast call is at 7:00AM followed by a second call at 8:00 AM. Lunch is served at 12:00 noon and again at 1:00 PM. Right after breakfast at 9:00AM, we muster to receive our daily combat assignments. Each of us "dog faced" guys is assigned to a sergeant with specific engagement orders. Sometimes we are ordered to exchange fire with the enemy and over run his position.

Other times we are ordered to take a hill and just observe and report on the enemy traffic on the road below. My primary job is to carry this 90-pound box of machine gun ammunition to the firing site. Carrying this 90-pound box of machine gun ammunition gets pretty heavy after a while. After carrying it for 10 or so miles and not using it, you feel like throwing it away. If you do engage the enemy, this box of ammo will last only a few minutes. What we need in this man's Army is a logistic system that will allow small amounts of heavy ammo to be carried by the GIs but have sufficient assets for a prolonged engagement. Many times, we are pinned down by Snipers and we are so far from our unit that we are all alone out there. To make a long story short we cannot get back to our unit for lunch. What we need is a snack we can take along to carry us over until we can reach home base. I do not mean one of these emergency meals. I would like some kind of sweet candy that would not melt all over the place in this hot summer heat." Mr.

Butter Payne continued, "Senator Knott Hurd I have friends stationed in the Hexagon that have access to the top brass. I passed this information along to my buddies. The logistics of the machine gun ammunition got lost in the shuffle. The top brass did pick up on the candy snack idea. Request for bids were let out to the candy manufactures. The candy snack must taste good, must not melt in a soldiers pocket, must contain a high energy to weight ratio, and must be packaged according to current sanitary practices. Each candy manufacturer is to fund the project with no help from the government. The patent and licensing agreements will be under the control of the manufacturer and not the military. It is anticipated that the military will consume 1,100,000 pounds of candy snacks per year.

Five candies manufacture submitted bids for the lucrative contract. The two leading bidders were the only ones seriously considered by the top brass in the Hexagon. Bidder number one took the approach of adding wheat fibers to the chocolate slurry until it met the heat resistant requirement. Bidder number two added filler to their existing milk chocolate and coated the small ball of chocolate with a hard sugar coating. Both manufactures met all of the requirements called out in the bid request. Most of the top brass were in favor of the sugar coated chocolate snack, which they called S&S's for Soldier and Sailor candy snack. They called the second snack HF's for High Fiber candy snack. A first vote among the top brass gave S&S a three to one lead over HF.

Now Senator Knott Hurd here is where the fun begins. The manufactures of HF hired Mr. Trotter Mudslinger a professional Lobbyist to represent HF during the contract negotiations. Mr. Mudslinger's main sales pitch was the high unemployment in the HF manufacturing area. During the war, cane sugar was hard to obtain for several reasons. The farmers did not like to use their limited resources to produce sugar while other products brought in more money. Some of our ammunition processing used large amounts of sugar. Cane sugar use soon become regulated and rationed by the Government. As a result, many of the commercial sugar users went out of business. Congresswoman Ankie Pankie is a strong supporter of the military. Her reelection will be in danger if the candy snack is not awarded to HF. If Congresswoman Ankie Pankie loses her seat in the House of Representatives, the Hexagon will lose a very dear friend. Congresswoman Ankie Pankie is working hard on the Anti-missile early detection appropriation bill.

Mr. Trotter Mudslinger's final words to the Hexagon top brass were, "You have a lot to lose by awarding the candy snack contract to S&S and not HF."

Well you know the rest. The contract was awarded to HF. HF is now out of business while S&S is still marketing their product under a different brand name. By the way, Senator Herd the HF candy snack was packaged into the emergency ration kit but most of the soldiers just threw it away.

The TV host concluded by saying that this is a true story. Senator Knott Hurd said, "I have heard of similar situations that happened during the war years. However, you know we had a gigantic logistical problem supplying 9,000,000 troops under combat conditions. It is no wander that some irregularities did occur. Mr. Butter Payne said," Senator it has been a pleasure having you on our show and I hope you can find time to do a return visit." Senator Hurd said, "It was my pleasure."

Business

Geraldine Neely had just finished her breakfast and was reading the morning newspaper. Her husband, Senator Samuel Neely, was still drinking the last bit of his coffee. Geraldine suddenly said, "Honey, I wish you would look here dear at this article in the newspaper. It shows the earnings of the top executives in the USA. Here is an oil company that made a 650 billion profit last year and the CEO made 2.4 million with a 1.5 million bonus. In addition, look here is another a telephone company made a profit of 2.1 billion and their CEO made 1.2 million. And look here is another auto company made a 200 billion profit and their CEO got 3.0 million bonuses." Sam replied," Yes, I know but I was just looking at the back of the page you are reading and it shows the companies that do not exist anymore and the ones going busted."

Geraldine continued, "I don't see why the CEO of a company should get those exuberant salaries and bonuses when all they do is set back in their easy chair and smoke expensive cigars. They all hire assistants to do the work that they should be doing. Really they don't do anything to earn that amount of money."

Sam again commented, "Well I disagree with you dear. On the back page, there are companies that are going broke and some of them are even out of business. The CEO's of these companies did not manage the assists of their company wisely. A CEO must keep abreast of the changing times. Take for instance the CEO of a buggy whip company of long ago. There is no market for buggy whips today. If the company did not adjust to the advent of the automobile then it probably is out of business today."

"Dear, let me read to you some of the remarks I made at the town hall meeting last year in Detroit. The CEO that can foresee the needs of customers in advance of others usually pushed his company ahead of others. The CEO that can do this is worth a lot of money. Sure, the CEO must surround himself with capable people but he ultimately must make the hard and tough decisions that make the company advance. If a CEO chooses "Yes, Yes" people for his staff then there is no room for fresh innovative ideas. The CEO must choose his staff wisely. Each employee must be loyal to the CEO but able to put forth new ideas freely. The CEO must be able to get the best out of each staff member in a tactful way."

"I am afraid that the successful CEO just does not set behind a desk and smoke expensive cigars. He is probably the hardest working employee in the organization. The CEO puts in more hours on the job than any other employee does. He is still on the job while at home and on vacation.

I have heard it said that that CEO made a lucky decision. Luck had little to do with it hard work is the answer. A few companies make a profit whether the economy is weak or strong. This is not just luck."

"The main reason these companies make a profit each quarter is good or excellent management. In each of this profit making organizations you will find a talented CEO. The CEO cannot make the economy go up or down but the CEO can adjust to the changing requirements of the changing environment. Let me quote from a speech I made last year at a town hall meeting in Ann Arbor."

"I remember when The Great Atlantic and Pacific Tea company (A&P) and Piggly Wiggly food stores were the best places to shop for groceries. In 1930, A&P had 16,000 stores with revenue of one billion dollars. A&P sold more goods than any other company in the world except for what General motors did. In 2008, the number of stores was down to 460. Piggly Wiggly had 2,660 stores in 1932 with total annual sales of $ 180 million. Today there are only 600 stores."

"Just a few years ago, the American Auto manufacturing industry was king. Today there is no American Motors Corporation (AMC). No Studebaker. No Packard, No Kiser Frasier, No Desoto. No Tucker.

What happened to these giant companies? Simple: the CEOs did not force the companies to adjust to the changing conditions. While other stores were failing, Samuel Walton opened a small Five and Dime store in a little town with a population of 34,000 in Arkansas. Today Wal Mart has 8,500 stores with a combined$ 258 billion in US sales."

"Do you remember the F. W. Woolworths & Co.? Do you remember the S. H. Kress & Co five and ten cent stores? At one time Woolworths had 807 stores. All stores were closed in 1981"

"Homebuilders have had a hard time during this last recession. Wall Homes, Breaking Home builders Group, Twin Cities, Orleans Homebuilders Gemcraft all have filed for bankruptcy."

Let us suppose that you are the CEO of a manufacturing company that makes auto hood ornaments. In the 1950's auto are selling well. Car companies are making lots of money. What is even better every auto had a hood ornaments on it. However, as time goes on some car body designers do not specify a hood ornaments in their design. The following year more cars are on the market without hood ornaments. Now is a good time to increase production of hood ornaments, build a second production facility, and hire 1000 new employees. Wrong. This sounds silly, but that is exactly what some CEO's have done."

"The summer before I went to college, when I was 18 years old, I went to work in a meat packing company. My boss would let me attend some of the Board of Directors meetings. He wanted me there to serve coffee and snacks to the other Board members. I remember one board meeting very well. The CEO of the company said that the company was going to package the wiener hot dogs in twelve unit boxes. He said that it would be easier to keep track of the number of hot dog wieners that way. One of the board members was also the marketing manager. He objected to the 12 pack. His point was that all of the hot dog buns manufactures packaged their product in eight unit packages. The CEO said that he did not give a damn what the bun manufacturers did we are going to package in 12 unit boxes. He had to purchase a new packaging machine. New 12 pack boxes were ordered and new printing was required. He built a 5,000 square foot addition to the building. All of this was paid for through a bank loan. Well our hot dog wieners remained on the grocer's shelves while the customer bought our competitor's hot dogs. The company could not make the payments on the bank loan and the company eventually went out of business. All because of a poor decision made by the CEO. Yes, It may appear that some CEO's are overpaid. On the other hand, Companies that have less capable CEO's may not make it through the tough times.

ANTI-LOBBYING-INITATIVE

When the TGHDC 9:00 AM military briefing ended at 9:30 AM, and all of the guests left the circular office, Damon Wineseller, the President's Political Advisor, remained seated. As the last person left the room, Damon said, "Mr. President I need to talk to you a few minutes." The President said, "Shoot." Damon said, "Mr. President I did a little research on the lobbying situation. In the last 90 days, there have been 1,246 US postal letters, 4,800 e-mails messages and numerous telephone calls. All of these communications are complaining of the lobbying condition at the capitol. I could not get a count on the number of phone calls, as the communications chief does not track phone calls by category. However, he did say the figure would run up into the thousands. Mr. President the people are fed up with the big corporations hiring lobbyist to pressure congressional representatives into spending money for their pet projects."

We have 1,268 registered lobbyists and who knows how many that are not registered, the estimate is about 4,000. It's about time that we brought the lobby machine to a standstill." The President committed, "I did not realize it was that serious of a problem, Damon." Damon stated, "Several of the congressmen have complained that their constituents' are very upset." The President said, "Ok that does it. I call an emergency meeting at 2:00 PM today and see what can be done about it." The President dialed "07" on his desktop communicator. Tom came running in and said, 'You called, Sir?' The President replied, "Yes, Tom, I want an emergency meeting setup to discuss the congressional lobby problem. I want the Speaker of the House, the Senate Majority Leader, the Senate Minority Leader all of my Cabinet, Yourself and of course Damon Wineseller to attend, ok. Get on it Tom."

At 2:02 PM, The president brought the meeting to order. He started the meeting by saying, "Our forefathers established many procedures and policies that have endured to this day. However, as we grow as a nation we must sometimes discard the old in favor of the new. The idea of lobbyist cajoling congressional representatives to pass laws that favor their rich clients must end. The voters have spoken and they are fed-up with the lobby concept. The mail, both hard copies in addition, electronic that is received in the GREY HOUSE DC each day is overwhelmingly against lobbying. I am not saying that lobbying is all-bad. There are some good sides to almost everything. Let me quote you some of the atrocities that have come to my attention. The defense department purchased 50 submarines that the navy did not want. All of this started out as HB-11009-A—rev B in the House. One hundred airplanes were bought for the air force that they cannot use. Again House Bill HB-10033-KK pushed by a lobbyist. The Army has 200 armored vehicles parked in the sand, as they are not suitable for combat. House Bill HB-12000-P was promoted by one of our lobbyist. A news reporter got a hold of this information and blasted it all over the country. Most of our voters do read, you know. If we do not fix this problem pronto, we will not be here after the next election. I do not know how to put this in a nice way. However, damn it I want action and I want it now. BANG, BANG, went the President's gavel, the meeting is adjourned.

The news of the President's emergency meeting spread through out the halls of congress and The GREY HOUSE DC. The lobbyists were the first to pick up on the news?

Freelance lobbyist Claude Hammer's face turned red and large blood vessels popped out on his neck. "What the hell does he think he is doing?" was his only remark. Claude Hammer called Tom and asked for a quick meeting with the President. The President had just finished a fast sandwich and he said, "Send the guy on over, Tom." Tom made his normal introduction, "Mr. President may I introduce Mr. Claude Hammer registered freelance lobbyist." The President said, "Thank you Tom, Please close the door behind you" The President continued, "Well Mr. Claude Hammer I have heard a lot about you" Claude Hammer said, "I want to thank you Mr. President for giving me this time out of your very busy schedule." The President responded, "What can I do for you Mr. Claude Hammer." Claude Hammer answered, "I understand that you are behind this "Anti-Lobby" initiative?" The President said, "from the number of postal letters, e-mail messages, and phone calls that the GREY HOUSE DC had received in the last few months I would say it is the will of the people to get rid of the lobbying machine." The President pressed, "07-A-03" on his desktop communicator. The, "07" is a call for Tom on both his desktop communicator and his portable belt pager. The, "A" puts the office conversation on Toms Desk top communicator. The, "03" is a secret code that means for Tom to listen but do not talk. Claude Hammer said, "Lobbying has been the American way of doing business in the capitol for years, Mr. President. Lobbying is an effective mechanism to get the will of the people across to congress. Without lobbying congress would be out of touch with the voters that put them in office in the first place." The President counters with, "Yes, but the big money guys always get first crack at any agenda they want to advance over the little guy. The little people lose out in our present lobbying system." Claude comes back with, "Mr. President, you are going against the grain on this one. I want you to know that I intend to fight you all the way on this imitative. I know that you raise a lot of money during your campaign tours and you like the system that allows you it do this. Well I am here to tell you that your campaign fund raising effort results in only a fraction of the money that passes through my hands I do not intend to see my business disappear. You know the courteous thing to do would be to consult me before you put in all of this effort. I am starting behind in this race, Mr. President but I will catch up I promise. I am not about to let you or anybody else destroy my way of life. We are going to have a lot of fun in this "Dog and Piney Show." Well Mr. President we both know how we stand on this issue may the best man win. I want to think you for your time, good day Mr. President." The President said, "Don't let the door slap you on the Butt on the way out, Mr. Claude Hammer." As Claude Hammer left the room, Tom entered. Tom said, "Looks like this is going to be all out war, Mr. President."

REELECT-SENATOR-CHISELER

The Reverend Homer Isa Bratt is the pasture of a small church that seats 256 people. His church if full of worshipers every Sunday. The attendance is around 300. Some people had to use temporary steel folding chairs while others stood and leaned up against the wall. The same thing happens each Wednesday at bible study class. The church is full. Members of the church, especially the younger ones, refer to the Reverend as Preacher Isa.

Some of his church leaders suggested that the Reverend seek the Senate seat now held by Mr. Ernest Chiseler. One of the offers in the church told the reverend that he should capitalize upon his popularity and run for office. With all of this encouragement to make the run, that is exactly what he did. In the evening, he would watch TV and learn what the other candidates were doing. He would then stand in front of his 6-foot tall mirror and mimic what he saw on TV.

The reverend would jump on any little fault he could see in the incumbent Senator. He was accustomed to raising money so purchasing TV ads were no problem. He was having a ball running down Senator Chiseler.

Many of the voters became confused with all of the negative newspaper ads and the depressing TV blitz. Several voters got together and promoted a candidates face-to-face show down.

Mr. Theodore Wolfe was appointed host, moderator, and organizer for the town Hall Meeting. The top four contenders were invited to speak. One of the contenders refused to be part of what he called political mud wrestling match.

The format for the candidate face-off was established. Each speaker would be allowed 10 minutes to state their agenda and tell why they should be the second Senator for the State. At the end of the candidates, presentation there would be a question and answer period. The Moderator would select questioners from the audience.

Senator Chiseler, the incumbent, was facing some fierce competition from his opponents. His major opponent is trying to paint the Senator as an evil man. In the Senator's address he pointed out several times that, his opponent had no political or administrative experience. The Senator's opponent is a Southern Baptist Preacher. The preacher did have more experience raising money than the Senator.

Host Theodore Wolf opened the meeting in the usual parliamentary manor.

The first question from the audience was from a woman on the front row. Here is her question, "Senator Chiseler my name is Mrs. Wright Nassy. I heard that your opponent call you a Muslim. Is that true?" The Senator responded, "Mrs. Nassy, I could answer your question with a simple no but I am not going to do so. The First Amendment to the Constitution guarantees me freedom of religion. My religious beliefs have nothing to do with my ability to serve this community as their Senator. I know that this is a very blunt answered but this is the way I feel. The monitor asked for another question.

The woman sitting right next to Mrs. Nassy raised her hand. The monitor gave her the portable microphone. She began, "Senator Chiseler is you a Mormon?" Senator Chiseler responded, "Well you did not give your name but I'll give the same answer to you as I gave to Mrs. Nassy. The first Amendment gives us all the freedom of religion.

The Host, Theodore Wolfe, again reiterated, when you ask our quest speakers a question, Please give your full name. Theodore Wolf announces, "Next Question Please." This questioner spoke up nice and loud into the microphone, "Senator Chiseler, my name is Mrs. Canna Spitz, are you Jewish?" Senator Chiseler Uttered, "Again It does not matter what religious affiliation a candidate has. My answer to your question is the same as before and any future questions about my religious beliefs will receive the same answer."

The next question came from a man on the second row. He said, "Senator Chiseler, My name is Maverick Builder, are you gay?" The Senator answered, "No"

Senator my name is Little Bear Walking. I am a Native American. I live in what you people call "The Indian Reservation." Senator you do not know what poverty is until you visit the so-called "Indian Reservation." Only three out of every 100 residents have permanent jobs. The three paychecks must sustain 100 residents. Oh yes, we do get a small check from the government, but it is not enough to buy food for a family of two. Some of our women folks sell Indian souvenirs made from ceramic dolls made in China.

They paint the doll faces with war paint add a few glass beads and some chicken feathers and sell them on the street at the entrance to the reservation.

We have one Doctor and two Nurse Practitioners to take care of the medical needs of over one thousand people. There is no dental facility on the reservation. There are no movie theaters or fast food restaurants. Two gasoline filling stations and a grocery store went out of business last year. The plastic button-molding factory closed two months ago. We lost 50 jobs when it closed. We have a cattle feed bagging operation and a dog food processing plant on the reservation. These two facilities are the only employment opportunities left for us.

Several years ago, an agent from the Cosmos National Bank came to the reservation and signed up 90% of the Native Americans for Visa credit cards. It was easy to go to the bank's ATM and withdraw cash. The next stop after the ATM usually was the liquor store for some men. We were not used to using plastic to make purchases. Soon the credit card balance reached the maximum of $9,000.00. There is no way that they can pay back that kind of money. Most of the cardholders have maxed out their credit cards at $9,000.00.

Our houses need painting and repair. The plumbing does not work. Some of our city streets are still dirt or gravel. Most of our old water wells are dry. There is very little wood left to heat our houses in the winter. The telephone service only works part time.

We have no public laundry facility. Our children are dressed in rags. There is no taxicab service on the reservation. Senator if you are reelected, what do you plan to do for us Native Americans?" The Senator Chiseler responded, "I am a very compassionate person. Your story is very touching. Little Bear your question is so broad that I can only give you a very broad answer. Please be more specific and state the problem you want me to address. Tell me what you suggest I do to help you. I will be glad to consider your request.

May I suggest that you get together with some of your fellow Native Americans and draft up a letter, state a specific problem, and suggest what I can do to help? Send the letter to my office in DC. Little Bear I know this not the answer you were looking to get from me. I cannot solve all of the world's problems with the wave of my hand. I can only work hard to change things for the better. Give me something that I can work on and I will do the best I can for you. The audience gave a generous round of applause for the Senator's Response.

Host Theodore Wolf queried, "Do we have a question for Reverend Homer Bratt?" Theodore recognized a woman on the third row. She said, "This question is for candidate Homer Bratt, she said, "My name is Miss Jolly Hummer, Mr. Brat I understand that you pay no income taxes yet you have over a million Dollars deposited in a Swiss Bank. The reverend Mr. Bratt Pronounced, "Honey, I don't know where you are getting your information you need the check out your information source. Jolly Hummer quickly quip,

"But Mr. Bratt you did not answer my question." Mr. Bratt said, "it is true I do not pay any income tax to the IRS and No, I do not have a million dollars in a Swiss bank."

Host Wolf asked for the next question. A woman in the center of the auditorium responded. "Reverend Bratt, My name is Mrs. Nazell Posie My friends call me Nosy Posy. There was a newspaper article about two years ago, that stated a Preacher

Bratt was caught in a police sting operation at a local brothel. How do you justify this reverend?" Reverend Bratt voiced, "There are Three Bratts in this town that preach the Gospel." Mrs. Nazell Posie asked, "You know that every aspect of your life will be put under the political microscope, is there anything that you are ashamed of doing?" The Reverend Bratt responded, "We all have little things hidden away in the closet that we do not wish to expose, but you have not touched upon one yet."

Host Wolf asked for the next question. A young woman stood up and answered, "Senator Chiseler, My name is Miss Lightly Frost. Do you believe the United States could elect a woman President? The Senator alleged, "Yes, Miss Frost, I do. And it will be within your life time."

A man on the second row responded to host Wolf's quest for another question. He spoke, "Senator Chiseler my name is Fermin Wett Barr. Senator is there any possibility that you will withdraw from the race?" The answer from the Senator was, "no sir, this is my business, this is my life I wouldn't know how to do anything else. Politics is the only thing I know how to do, Sir."

Mr. Wolf asked for another question. A woman was recognized and allowed to speak. She voiced, "Senator my name is Miss Closs Shaver, and my question to you is this. Senator if you were offered a major position in the administration would you resign your senate seat. The Senator reported, "That is a difficult question to answer. It would depend upon what position you had in mind; also I don't think the offer is very likely."

Host Wolf asked for another question. A man raised his hand for the second time. He was recognized by the host. He said, "Reverend Brat I still don't know why you think you are qualified to be a Senator in the United States congress." Reverend Bratt pronounced, "I am as qualified as any one running in this race. You do not go to school to learn how to be a Senator. You learn on the job. You listen to the advice of your peers. You must have an honest desire to serve. What more do you want Mr. Maverick Builder?"

Reverend Bratt thanked the group for having him here to express his views on some touchy subjects. A young woman in the center of the auditorium raised her hand. She was recognized by host Wolf. She uttered, "Reverend Bratt, my name is Miss Anita Hart Buster, "I was just thinking, Reverend if the battle in the congress gets down right vulgar do you think you can stand the heat of the kitchen as Truman once said?" The Reverend Bratt alleged, "Miss Buster, We all face difficult and trying time as go down life's pathway. Nobody said that life would be smooth and easy.

Yes, there is a lot of heat in the kitchen and sometimes there is a lot of heat the congressional debates. This is part of the game. Miss Buster I think I have enough strength and will power to withstand the turmoil in congress. Does that answer your question?" Miss Buster answered, "Yes, It did, Reverend Bratt."

Host Wolf recognized young women in the far back of the auditorium she stood up and proclaimed, "Senator, My name is Mrs. Rofasha Cobb, I am a naturalized citizen from India. I voted for you last time. Senator what I would like to know is this. "Senator if you are re-elected what do you plan to do differently next time that you didn't do this term?" Senator Chiseler voiced, "That's a pretty easy question to answer, Rofasha. You see Congress is a breathing living thing nothing is ever the same. You have to meet the challenges as they come your way. The same problem today that you had yesterday may require a different solution. You ask what I would do different; well I will do whatever is required. Did that answer your question, Rofasha?" Rofasha nodded her read and replied, "I think so."

Host Wolf asked, "Are there any questions for the reverend?" A man raised his hand and was recognizes. He said, "Reverend Bratt, my name is Littlejohn Mendoza. I want to know if elected can you keep your religious feelings out of the country's business."

Homer Bratt's response was, "Littlejohn, My religion is part of me and I cannot separate it from the rest of me, However if you are worried that I will let my religious feelings interfere with running the country you can forget it."

Host Wolfe recognized a woman on the fourth row. She began, "Reverend Bratt my name is Miss Alice King Foote or A King Foote. I am an Elementary school teacher. My students call me "Aching Foot." I know that the first amendment to the constitution gives us freedom of religion. We can practice any religion that we choose. There are many different religions in this world. Some of these religions have elements that seem to conflict with elements in other religions. My question is how you see members of congress working together having different religious points of view. Let us suppose you are the head of the 'World Relief' food committee. On your committee are a Protestant, a Catholic, a Jew, a Mormon, Muslin, a Hindu, and an Atheist. Do you think you could get a common group agenda from this committee?

The Reverend Bratt answered, "Miss Foote, There are differences in the religions of the world. There are differences in each of us yes; I think we can all work together.

Host Wolf asked for one final question. A man on the front row stood up and began to speak, "Senator Chiseler my name is Le Roy Larkin Goode you are not as liberal as some people on the left or as conservative as some people on the right, have you ever thought of switching parties?

The Senator gave one last deep breath and replied, "No, sir I have not."

Senator Chiseler thanked the audience for their atheistic participation and for asking some interesting questions. He said, "The audience and my opponent probed deeply to find little hidden secretes in my past.
As the reverend said earlier and I quote, "Everyone has some skeletons in their closets but you have not found one yet. Unquote." Thank you very much"

The reverend Homer Bratt thanked the audience and said, "See you at the poles."

The host Theodore Wolf thanked everyone for their participation in the town hall meeting. He also announced that the minutes of this meeting would appear in next week's newsletter. "Have a safe drive back home."

Karen Berkowitz-Secretary of Defense

Steven Boyd, Congressman in the House of Representatives from one of the southern gulf coast states corners Karen at the food buffet. Karen is trying to balance her food tray and a scotch and water drink analog with her desert in one hand and French handbag in the other hand. Steven offered to carry her drink to the table. They both went through their food along with three more drink servings. About half way through the meal the band started to play and Steven asked if she would like to do the waltz. It was not long until Karen said, "You can hold me a little closer. I am afraid I might fall. Those scotch and waters are getting to me. When they sat down at the table after the dance Steven brought her another scotch and water. Karen began to relax and stretched her legs straight out from under the table. She let out a whee-oou and said, "My feet are killing me." Steven said, "may be a good foot rub would be in order?" Karen replied that would be nice, Steven." Steven answered, "I've been told that I am a pretty good foot massager." Karen said, "you know I might just take you up on that." Steven said, "let's get a drink for the road, I'll get a room upstairs and we'll see just how good I am, OK?" One more scotch, water, a gin and tonic, and they were on their way up stairs.

Once in the room, Karen removed her shoes. Steven gave each foot a gentle massage. After about half an hour Karen said, "That's enough Steven. I do not want you to get too excited. Steven said, "Sure thing. Now I have a little request to make of you. You know that my congressional district has a submarine building facility on the coast. The unemployment rate is twice the national average. I need to get some orders for subs or I may be voted out of office. If I'm voted out you won't get any more foot rubs." Steven continued, "What I need is for you to approve the requisition for 50 of my new sub marines I know that the Navy has said that they do not need them, but what do the Admirals know. Karen said, "We need another drink." Steven called room service and ordered another round of drinks. When the drinks arrived, Karen and Steven got very comfortable each in their individual easy chair. When the last drop of the drinks were consumed they drifted off to sleep.

Congressman Rowland Watermulen-THM

The town hall meetings are a very important instrument in our political system. The meeting between the politician and the voters that he or she represents gives an excellent opportunity to exchange views on the issues concerning all involved. The politician can use the meeting as a platform to get across to the voters the agenda he or she wishes to sell. The voters have a chance to voice some of the concerns that trouble them. It need not go to say that all town hall meetings go smoothly. In fact, some town hall meetings become very turbulent or even ballistic. The management of a town hall meeting requires a lot of personal skill. Having said this we will examine some of the fictional goings on at town hall meetings.

At last month's meeting of the local chapter of the American Association of Independent Political Views Union (AAIPVU), one of the items of new business was to have a town hall meeting in the little town of Swankersville. Mr. Claude Snapper, the president of the local chapter of the AAIPVU was appointed Host and Moderator of the proposed town hall meeting. Notices were posted into the newspaper and advertising time was purchased on the AM radio station. The hall began to fill up at 1:00 PM for the scheduled 2:00 PM meeting.

Mr. Claude Snapper, the president and host brought the meeting to order at exactly 2:00 PM. His first words were, "Good afternoon members of the AAIPVU, visitors, and guests. We will have a very short business meeting before we hear our honored guest speaker.

First, we will have a prayer by the reverend Froglegg Clearstone, the secretary will read the minutes of our last meeting, and the treasurer will give a financial report. All of the old business has been taken care of and there is no new business. I will then turn the meeting over to our guest speaker Congressman Rowland Watermulen. The meeting was short indeed only 10 minutes long. Claude Snapper introduced Congressman Rowland Watermulen by saying," Congressman we all are anxiously awaiting your comments on the upcoming legislation that will affect our community here in the second congressional district. However, most of all we await your response to the questions from the floor.

Having said that, "Ladies and gentlemen I give you Congressman Rowland Watermulen Congressional representative from the second district. Claude Snapper officiated during the question and answer period. He kept order in the house with his firm business like decorum.

Congressman Rowland Watermulen did not say anything that might pin him down. There were no firm commitments on the things he should be doing when he gets back to DC. The interesting part of the meeting came during the question and answer period after the town hall meeting speech.

Congressman Rowland Watermulen has just finished his pitch for fiscal responsibility in the Government. At the end of his speech, he asked for questions from the audience. A woman raised her hand. She was recognized. She began by saying, "Senator, My name is Crystal Clear and I have a question for you."

At this point, the congressional representative interrupted saying, "Excuse me Crystal Clear but I am not a Senator. I am a Representative from the second congressional district in this State. I am a member of Congress." Crystal Clear continued, "Sorry Congressman, but it's hard to tell a Senator from a Congressional representative these days. My question sir is this, Can anything be done to keep our good paying jobs here in the United States and not let them be shipped overseas? If the jobs were still here and people were paying taxes we would not be in the mess we are in right now." Congressman Watermulen responded, "That is a good question Crystal Clear. It has been the policy in the federal government for several years to promote free trade. Some folks say that we have gone too far in the free trade direction. When I get back to Washington, I will propose that a study panel be formed to address this very question. I know this was not a very good answer to your question Crystal Clear but it is the best I can do right now."

Claude Snapper asked, "Can we have another question please?"

A man raised his hand. The man was recognized by the host. "Congressman, my name is Billy Cole Burnner and I have a question for you. I do not smoke. My parents did not smoke. When I go into a building where smoking is prohibited, the area around the door way smells like a garbage can from the stale cigarette smoke. I know that cigarette smoke causes cancer and the second hand smoke cannot be good for your health. Yet I am forced to inhale stale cigarette smoke almost every day.

I try to stay away from smokers but that is almost impossible to do. The big problem I have is that my girlfriend smokes like a freight train. When I kiss her, it is like kissing the toilet seat. I have to take breath mints after kissing her. I chew gum all the time I am with her." The audience began to snicker.

Congressman Rowland Watermulen interrupted by saying, "That is an awful sad story Mr. Burnner, but what can I do to help?" The audience let out a loud chuckle. "Well you see Congressman Watermulen there is a pretty stiff tax on cigarettes already. However, if this tax was raised about 10 times what it is now many smokers would quite the habit. I know my girlfriend could not afford the higher cost. What

I would like you to do is to introduce a bill in Congress that would put a federal tax on cigarettes of $10.00 per pack." Again the audience gave out a big laugh.

"Well Mr. Billy Cole Burnner the problem of getting that kind of bill through Congress is much like your trying to dodge the smokers. There are so many smokers in Congress that a bill to increase cigarette tax would have no chance of passing." Congressman Watermulen asked, "Have you tried hiding your girlfriend's cigarettes?" The audience gave forth another round of laughter. Congressman Watermulen said, "I understand your problem but I do not think there is anything I can do for you at the federal level. Think you for your question."

Claude Snapper announced, "Next Question, Please." Claude recognized a man standing in the back of the room. He spoke, "Congressman Watermulen my name is Mr. T. Bird Driver. You said in your speech that you would keep Social Security and Medicare the same as it is now. You also said that you would not increase taxes and that you would reduce the federal deficit. You said earlier that you are in favor of increasing the armed forces defense budget. Congressman just how are you going to accomplish all of this?" Congressman Watermulen answered, "Well mister T. Bird that is a very good question and it is one that many people are asking these days. You see Mr. Driver the fiscal activity of the federal government is much like your finances at home. Do you have a budget at your house mister Driver?"

Mr. T. Bird Driver responded, "Yes Sir I do." Congressman Watermulen said, "You work and bring in money to the household. You have certain fixed expenses like mortgage payments, electric and telephone bills. You also have certain variable expenses like new tires for the car, Johnnie's new bicycle, and entertainment. After you pay the fixed expenses, let us say you have $500.00 dollars left over. New tires cost $400.00 Johnnie's bicycle costs $100.00. Wife's new evening outfit costs $ 600.00 two evening meals at the restaurant costs $140.00. A new propeller for the boat costs $80.00. Mr. T. Bird you can see that the $500.00 dollars left over after the fixed expenses will not buy all of the things on your wish list. You have two alternatives. You can cut back on the number of items on your wish list or you can go in debt and buy some items on a credit card. Does that make since Mr. Driver?" "Yes, all of that sounds familiar." answered Mr. Driver "Well the Federal Government behaves much in the same way. There are certain items that the law requires to be funded just like the fixed items in your budget.

Now we come to the variable federal government expenses. We could say look there just is not enough money to go around so we have to cut out some of the variable expense items. An alternative action would be to issue new US Treasury certificates and use the money from the sale of the certificates to buy the variable expense items. This last action is similar to your credit card purchases. There is one big problem with this last choice. Eventually this borrowed money must be paid back. Where is the money going to come from to repay the debt? That is pretty simple just issue more US Treasury Certificates and use the money from the sale of the certificates to repay the first batch of certificate holders. You may say that this sounds somewhat stupid. Well that is what the government has been doing for the last 50 years. You asked how I would fix this huge problem. The federal Government just like your household. It must live within the established budget. This means that some very tough decisions must be made. You simply cannot have your cake and eat it too. Our expenditures must not exceed our income. There should be some money left over to help pay down our run away national debt. Does that answer your question Mr. T. Bird Driver?" Mr. T. Bird Driver answered, "Yes, Congressman Watermulen, I it does. I guess there is no simple answer to this question."

The next member to respond the Host's quest for questions from the audience was a young woman just recently moved into the second congressional district.

Here is what she had to say. "Congressman Rowland Watermulen my name is Miss Iona Sockque. I would like to thank you personally for being able to spend some time with us. I think all representatives should take the time to get to know the needs of your constituents. Congressman Watermulen I have three very large rosemary bushes in my front yard next to the common sidewalk. We have an ordinance in our town that states pets must be on a leash at all times. About 90 percent of the pet owners carry a little plastic bag to retrieve the solid waste that their pet leaves as they stole down the sidewalk. Male dogs like to mark the trees and bushes as the walking exercise progresses. The problem is that I use the rosemary whenever I cook chicken. Sure, I wash the rosemary before using but the thought of dog urine in my food is revolting. This is not an isolated case in the second congressional district. I have relatives in Michigan, Texas, Florida, and Arizona. I have friends in Ohio, Tennessee, Virginia, and Oregon. Each of these places has the same problem. Since the issue is not a local one, it must be addresses on the federal level. What I am asking you to do is to introduce a bill in congress to make it a federal offence to let your pet urinate on someone else's property. Therefore, Congressman Rowland Watermulen when you get back to DC and you do not have anything else to do, think up a bill that will keep the dog urine out of my food. Thank you very much."

Congressman Watermulen responded, "Miss Iona Sockque. I do not think a bill kike the one you suggested would ever get through the Congress. I will run it by my staff when I get back to DC and see what they think."

Host Claude Snapper announced, "Do we have another question?" A Native American answered the Host's call for questions. "Sir my name is Standing Tree John. I am a Native American. I vote in the second congressional district. In this state, there are many Native Americans. Some people refer to us as Indians. It seems that when Columbus set sail for India back in 1492 He ran into North America and he thought that he had reached India. He called us Native Americans Indians. We do not mind however, we prefer to be called Native Americans.

Congressman Watermulen, You can see that my eyes are tearing up even before I begin to speak. You see Congressman Watermulen we Native Americans worship the majestic mountains, the rich green forest, the free clear running water and the tall evergreen trees. There is a place where two small creeks come together and make one larger creek. It is at this place where my family, my friends, and I come to worship. We give thanks for the great mountains towering up above us and for the majestic green forest, but mostly for the pure clear running water in the creek. As we pray and look at the beautiful mountains, we see a giant bulldozers carving away at the mountain surface. They are making roads and building structures on our sacred mountains. They bring in rock from the riverbed to pave the roads. These rocks do not belong on the mountain. There is an old Indian Saying: 'If you move a stone or rock from its original birth place. Thunder and lightning will come and the storm will consume you.'

Builders like to build nice homes made of wood. The wood comes from trees. The trees come from our forest. Our forest is being destroyed tree by tree to build these fine homes.

As we look out across the creek, we see an old discarded refrigerator, part of an old cook stove, and seven worn out automobile tires. There are two sacks in the creek of who knows what inside. Down the creek, a little ways is an old rusted out car body and two old bicycle tires.

Congressman Watermulen we Native Americans do not try to destroy your God and place of worship. Then why do you insist upon turning our objects of worship and place for giving thanks into a garbage dump?

Congressman Watermulen please look into my eyes and see the tears as they roll down my cheek and fall from my chin onto the floor. I know that when you get back to DC you will have forgotten the words that I have spoken. However, maybe you can remember my tearful face and try to help us. Thank you Congressman Watermulen for your time."

As Standing Tree John concluded, there was a great roar from the audience and tremendous applause as he took his seat. Congressman Watermulen said, "Standing Tree John that was the most moving speech that I have heard since I've been in the political arena. However, you are wrong about one thing. I will not forget the words you spoke here tonight. They are burnt into my heart and I promise you that I will do everything in my power to rectify the damage that civilization has done to your way of life. In addition, I will never forget the tearful look on your face as you spoke. Thank you Standing Tree John for a very moving presentation."

Claude asked for another question. "Congressman Watermulen, my name is Rusty Gunn Calhoun. My property line butts up against the Greasystone National Park. We have an ecology unbalance problem in the park. The ground in the park next to me is as hard as cement. When it rains, the rainwater just runs off to the creek. The trees and other vegetation do not get enough water to sustain life. Normally the ground should be soft and porous with lots of loam and plenty of earthworms. Normally the earthworms make little holes that let the rainwater go down to feed the roots to the vegetation. Grub worms do the same things. The rotting twigs and other old vegetation help the earth retain the rainwater. Other earth boring creatures help the soil retain water.

You see the problem is that the mice, rats, and snakes eat the earthworms and grub worms. The hawks and buzzards eat the nice, rats, and snakes. The very bad winter storms last year destroyed the habitat of the buzzards and hawks. There are fewer hawks and buzzards than a normal balanced ecology will require. If the buzzards and hawks are not eating the nice, rats and snakes then there are more nice, rats, and snakes than a normal balanced ecology demands. The nice, rats, and snakes are eating all of the earth worms and grub worms." Congressman Watermulen interrupted by saying," OK, Rusty that is an interesting story but what does it have to do with this town hall meeting?" Rusty replied, "Senator the park is government property and we voters expect the government to take care of it in a proper way."

The Congressman spoke, "Hold on Rusty, I am a US congressional representative from the second congressional district, not a Senator. Rusty, specifically what do you want me to do." "Congressman Watermulen I want you to put forth a bill in congress to either import into the park more buzzards and hawks or set traps to reduce the nice, rat, and snake population. I don't think this is an unreasonable request." At this point, the audience busted out into laughter. Congressman Watermulen Asked, "Mr. Rusty Gunn Calhoun would you be willing to go to a congressional meeting and let me introduce you and you give the pitch I just heard?" Rusty Gunn Calhoun said," no Congressman I would not, I voted for you to represent me in Congress and I expect you to do so,"

Claude Snapper signaled for the sergeant at arms to come forward and escort Rusty out of the meeting. A loud applause could be heard as the sergeant at arms and Rusty left the auditorium. Congressman Rowland Watermulen said, "you sure do have some lively meetings here at the Independent Voter Union Association. Claude Snapper thanked the Congressman for his smooth control of the situation.

Claude Snapper asked, "Do we have another question."

A man on the third row raised his hand. He was recognized. The host brought the portable cordless microphone to him. The man began by saying. "Congressman Watermulen, my name is Bozoleni Gotsoleni. My friends call me BOZO.

My pet peeve is the deceptive advertising and misleading labels I see every day. For instance, Toilet paper has nothing to do with the toilet. Bathroom tissue has nothing to do with the bathroom. All of these are for the butt and should be called butt paper." Bozo made a final gesture by standing up with the portable microphone in his right hand and a half-full pint of bourbon in his left hand. As he raised both hands above his head, he fell forward across the chair in front of him and into the woman's lap in that chair. The host rushed to the podium, seized the microphone from the podium stand, and announced, "Will the sergeant-at arms please remove the drunken BOZO from the auditorium." When the Congressman regained control of the microphone he announced, "Boy, We sure do have some exciting times here in the second congressional district."

Claude Snapper asked for another question. A woman seated in the seat directly behind the seat that Bozo sat in raised her hand. She was recognized by Host Claude Snapper. She began to speak, "Congressman Watermulen, My name is Mrs. Regenia Ricobugy. I vote in the second Congressional District. Speaking of deceptive labeling, let me tell you what happened to me. Last July we had some friends over for the Fourth of July holiday. Just unexpectedly, we decided to have a hot dog BBQ. I went to the store and put two packages of hot dog wieners into my shopping cart. I headed over to the bread rack where I saw a large sign that read Package of eight hot dog buns for $1.89. I placed two of these packages into my shopping cart and headed for the Checkout cashier. When she rang up my hot dog buns, the register showed $2.39 per package. I immediately questioned the clerk by saying the sales price on the buns is $1.89 per 8-piece package. The clerk said, "Oh, That sale went off a month ago. I suggested that she call the Manager over to the cash register. The clerk told the manager that I wanted the old sales price on the hot dog buns. The Manager replied, "Oh that sale went off over a month ago. I explained that the sales price tag of $1.89 was still on the buns. The Manager and I walked over to the bread rack and I pointed out the large sales price sticker. The manager said, "Yes the buns were $1.89 but the sale expired on May 30. He further said that I must read all of the sales notice. Sure enough on the very bottom right hand corner, was a note in very small print saying the sale was good through May 30?

The Sales notice was printed in font size 72 and the sales termination notice was in size six font.

I too would like to see a federal law stating that all conditions, exclusions, and disclaimers are in the same font size as the sales pitch. Now retailers are allowed to deceive the public consumers without fear of prosecution." Congressman Watermulen responded, "Mrs. Ricobugy, I have had several complaints regarding deceptive labeling. When I get back to DC, I will ask my staff to investigate and probably write up a draft resolution to correct this problem. Thank you Mrs. Ricobugy for your question." Host Claude Snapper asked for another question.

"Congressional representative Watermulen my name is Miss Iwanda Samoura. I am a naturalized citizen of the United States born in the Philippians. Speaking of small print, I have right here in my hand a free coupon for two aluminum clad cork coasters. These coasters will protect my highly polished furniture from damage caused by hot or cold beverages. Again, they are free. Let me read to you the very small print at the bottom of the free coupon. I have to use a twenty-power magnifying glass to make out the words. I quote, 'you must activate the coupon by joining our premium gift club. The entrance fee for the premium gift club is $ 50.00. In order for our premium gift club members to receive the free aluminum clad cork coasters, you must agree to purchase twelve of our cane fiber ironing pads. These cane fiber-ironing pads normally sell for $ 9.95 each, but as a club member, you pay only $4.99 each. That is a 50% savings for our club members.'

Now Congressman Watermulen I ask you how free are those aluminum clad cork coasters. Fifty dollars to join the club and sixty dollars for twelve ironing pads I do not need and I get two coasters. Congressman we need to stop this kind of false advertising. By the way, the free coaster coupons were sent to me via the US mail. That makes it a federal issue. Now what are you going to do about it?"

Congressman Watermulen responded to Miss Iwanda Samoura statements, "I have received several complaints about small print on this trip. It appears that it is a wide spread issue, Yes, If these unscrupulous advertisers are using the United States Postal Service it could become a federal issue. When I get back to DC, I will ask a committee to investigate this situation."

Claude Snapper asked, "Can we have another question please?"

A woman near the center of the auditorium raised her hand. She was recognized by the Host Claude Snapper. She began to speak, "Congressman Watermulen, my name is Miss Slest Poole, I have here in my hand an empty carton that did contain 100% pure orange juice. Down at the very bottom of the carton are some small letters saying that the juice was made from concentrate. I order to bring orange juice concentrate back up to the normal PH water has to be added. Now we have water added to our 100% pure orange juice. If it is 100% orange juice it cannot have water added. We need more federal oversight on the labeling of products that are shipped to more than one State. What say you Congressman?"

Congressman Watermulen replied, "As I have said before I will investigate when I get back to DC."

Host Claude Snapper asked for another question. Another woman in the center of the auditorium raised her hand to be recognized.

"Congressman Watermulen, my name is Miss Upure Haas. I live in the second largest city in the second congressional district. Six years ago, we installed a lawn water sprinkler system in our large front yard. Our beautiful lawn is the envy of the neighborhood. The water for the sprinkler system comes from the city municipal water system. The city buys its water from the Waterloo Pumping station. Waterloo gets its water from the river. The river water goes through one of three large sedimentation tanks. From there the water goes through a series of filters before it enters the Waterloo pumping station building. The water is processed further inside the building. There are several Quality Control check stations inside the building. I understand that there 60 employees working at the Waterloo pumping station. One year after we installed our lawn water sprinkler system, the city raised our water rate 10%. Two years after that they raised out water rate another 15%. The following year the city raised our water rate another 15%. We decided to put in water well and not use the city water. The well is 800 feet deep and supplies all the water we need including the lawn sprinkler requirements.

The city municipal water people became suspicious when we stopped buying their water. They came to our house and after looking around asked how we were getting our water. We told them that we put in a deep well system. We did this because the water bill was getting too high." The water people asked, "Are you still hooked up to the city sewer system?" We told them that we were. They said, "You pay for the sewer service according to the amount of city water you use. If you are not paying for city water, you are getting your sewer service free. This has to stop. Besides this, you are using water from the same aquifer that the city uses. You must stop using this water."

"Congressman Watermulen the water stream underground runs through several different states. This makes the control of the underground water supply a federal issue and is not under local jurisdiction. What I want is a Federal law governing the use of underground water and prohibiting local governments from restricting its use."

Congressman Watermulen said, "You raise some very interesting points Miss Haas. I have never thought of a water supply as a federal issue. You are right, if the water runs through more than one State it must be a federal concern. Let me thank you Miss Haas for enlightening me on this issue. I will bring this up with my staff and see what we can do for you."

Host Claude Snapper announced, "We have time for just one more question. Congressman Rowland Watermulen has to catch a plane back to DC and it leaves in about one hour from now."

"Congressman Watermulen my name is MRS. Lacy Dodge Driver.

You met my ex-husband Mr. T. Bird Driver a few moments ago. My complaint is about the high cost of drugs. I understand that Drug companies must spend a lot of money to develop new drugs.

I also know that the patent protection runs out in about 7 years. At that time, other drug manufacturers market a generic equivalent drug to the original brand name.

The generic equivalent drug usually costs about one-sixth the cost of the brand name drug. What I cannot see is why the selling price of the brand name drug remains high even after the drug manufacturer has recovered the research, development and testing costs of the drug. We need a law to stop this racketeering of drug companies." Congressman Watermulen responded, "Mrs. Driver, if the drug company profits appear to be absorbent yes, we need to look at government regulations. The drug companies just like Ford and General Motors are in business to make a profit. Most of this so-called profit is distributed to the shareholders. The shareholders' money was used in the first place to fund the company's operation. If you greatly reduce the drug company's shareholder's return on investment, then these investors will look at other investment opportunities. Yes, Mrs. Driver we do need some federal government oversight on drug company's profits. We have such an organization in operation as we speak. It is the duty of Congress to monitor the effectiveness of this organization." Congressman Watermulen said, "Does that answer your question even though it is not the answer you would like to receive from me?" Mrs. Driver said, "Yes, and thank you very much."

Host Claude Snapper said, "Congressman Rowland Watermulen we wish to thank you for being our guest here today. You gave answers to some very interesting questions from our audience. We will be looking forward to another meeting with you in the very near future. Thanks again Congressman Rowland Watermulen."

Swankersville Town Hall Meeting
Ferguson & Epstein

The little town of Swankersville rest on the boundary between congressional districts two and six. Due to a mix-up in scheduling two Congressional representatives were scheduled to speak at the same time and same place. Congressman Ernest Ferguson from district six and Congressman Thomas Epstein from district two. These two men are good friends and have essentially the same political views. A town hall meeting was arranged by the local newspaper at the request of some of confused voters. A room was set up in the public library for this meeting. The meeting was posted in the newspaper. Congressman Ernest Ferguson was invited to explain some of his controversial stands on some important issues. Congressman Thomas Epstein was invited to explain his goals and objectives as a newly elected congressional representative. The meeting got under way at the scheduled time. The local barber acted as the meeting moderator. He introduced Congressman Thomas Epstein and the Congressman began his speech. Congressman Epstein rattled on for a good twenty minutes but did not say anything of any importance. The audience seemed happy just to hear the Congressional Representative speak.

The host then introduced Congressman Ernest Ferguson and the Congressman began to speak. Congressman Ferguson stated his position on several subjects. He covered stem-cell research, abortion, illegal immigration, border security, nuclear missile reduction, exporting our good jobs overseas, the national debt, and our sick economy. His main empathies however were on the need to stop global warming. The host thanked Congressman Ferguson for clearing up some of the misunderstandings and said, "Although we all do not agree with some of your positions at least we know where you stand."

When Congressman Ernest Ferguson finished his prepared speech on the need to stop global warming, the host asked the audience if they had any questions or concerns at this time. A young woman sitting on the front row rushed up to the host who was standing in front of the podium and snatched the portable microphone from his hands. She said, "Congressman Ferguson my name is Mrs. Lavender Bleach. I would like to see some federally sponsored regulations on traffic laws." Congressman Ferguson asked, "Mrs. Bleach is you sure this is federal issue?" Mrs. Bleach responded, "Yes, Your honor, please let me continue. I received a citation for speeding. I was told by the traffic officer that I was going 55 MPH in a posted 35 MPH zone I do not deny the fact that I was going over the posted speed limit. The officer told me that one of the methods of taking care of the speeding ticket was go to a certified traffic school. I searched the internet for a certified traffic school as suggested on one of the traffic ticket attached instruction sheets. I found a class that met the following Saturday morning at 7:00 AM. I was not sure of the address or how to get to the traffic school. I decided to drive to the traffic school today so that I would not have a problem early Saturday morning. The paper work that came with the traffic ticket stated that if I got a second traffic ticket within 24 months of the first one I would not be able to have it Excused by way of attending a certified traffic school. I was determined not to exceed the speed posted on the maximum speed limit signs. I was driving down the freeway at exactly 65 MPH the posted max speed limit on my way to the certified traffic school. Cars were passing me on both sides. The normal traffic flow on this part of the freeway is just less than 80 MPH. In my rear view mirror, I saw a van approaching at a high rate of speed.

He applied his brakes and swerved to the left to avoid rear-ending my car. By the time, he was squarely in the lane to the left of me his speed had decreased considerably. He was rear ended by a loaded speeding pick-up truck.

The investigating accident officer gave me a citation for driving too slow on the freeway and creating a traffic hazard. Your honor I was driving at the posted speed limit of 65 MPH. The normal traffic flow is around 80 MPH. We need some guidelines from the federal government that will prevent this kind of injustice."

Congressman Ferguson replied, "Mrs. Bleach, I do understand your problem. Your request is very unusual. I do not know if I can help or not. I will talk to the Lawyers on my staff and see if we can help you. Mrs. Bleach this best answer I can give you at this time."

The barber host asked, "Can we have a question for Congressman Thomas Epstein?"

The Host recognized a man on the first row. "Congressman Epstein my name is Mr. Coffin Slobber. I am sick and tired of these damn Federal Government Give-Away programs. I am specifically peeved at the government welfare programs. Congressman Epstein just where you think the money you are giving away is coming from. Let me tell you, it is my money that I pay to the IRS in Income Tax. I want Welfare stopped immediately. You are giving my money to able-bodied men and women that are too lazy to work. I want the Government to take the money that is now going for welfare checks and create jobs for every one that wants to work. To start with, the welfare administrator will offer a job to a qualified welfare recipient, if the welfare recipient refuses to work the welfare check is stopped immediately. Eventually the government will guarantee a job to any one that wants to work, and then there will be no more welfare."

Congressman Epstein replied, "Mr. Slobber your plan sounds rather socialistic to me." Mr. Slobber interrupted, "Well Congressman, don't you think our present welfare system is just a little bit socialistic?" The Congressman continued, "Mr. Slobber you have a point there. However, I have items that are more important on my agenda. To buck the well-established system of welfare would be non-productive. I promise you Mr. Slobber if I run out of things to I will jump on it. Thank you for your question."

The barber host asked for a question for Congressman E. Ferguson.

"Congressman Ferguson my name is Mr. Ohmar Lord. As you can see, I am on crutches. I need crutches to stand and to walk. I can drive a car but I have a difficult time getting in and out of my car. I do not have handicap license plates as my daughter drives me shopping in her car therefore I use the plastic handicap card that goes on the rear view mirror. My complaint is that Many times all handicap parking spaces are occupied by other cars that have handicap stickers but the occupants are not handicap at all. The other day a car cut me off and took the only handicap parking space left in the parking lot. Both occupants jumped out of the car and ran into the fast food restaurant. I stayed in my car, as I had to count my change. Soon both of the car occupants next to me came running out of the fast food store and blasted off in the handicap car. The car had out of State license plates. I would like to see the misuse of handicap parking a federal offence and punishable by a mandatory heavy fine." Congressman Ferguson said, "I never thought of parking lot regulation as being a federal government issue. I will run it by my staff when I get back to DC. Thank you for your question."

A woman in the very back of the Library meeting room raised her hand. She was accepted as the next questioner. The woman did not stand up but spoke setting in her wheel chair. She Said, "Congressman Ferguson, my name is Mrs. Lass Paige, I don't know what you can do to help me but let me tell you my story. I am crippled and in a wheel chair. The Doctors say I have Myasthenia Gravis. My arms are so week that propelling the chair by myself is very difficult. My primary Doctor sent me to a diagnostic imaging clinic to get an x-ray of my crippled legs and hip. I called a local senior citizen transportation service to take me to and from the x-ray facility. My x-ray appointment was at 1:15 PM. I told the telephone receptionist this on my first call to the transportation service. The driver of the transportation service's van arrived at my house at exactly 1:15 PM. A hectic 10-minute trip to the diagnostic imagining facility put me there at 1:25 PM. I explained the reason for my being late to the receptionist. She said she would try to work me in between other appointments. I told this to the driver and he said he could not wait and that I should call the office when the x-ray was finished. I was able to get my x-ray in about 45 minutes. I called the transportation service office and told them I was ready to go home. One hour and one half later the driver showed up to take me back home. The driver had a very poor attitude as he was working past his go-home time. He told me that his shift ended at 3:00 PM and it was now 3:40 PM. I told him that I had to wait in the lobby for one and a half hours for him to come and get me. He grabbed a hold of my wheel chair handles and gave them a violent jerk as we started to leave the x-ray facility.

I told him, "Hey, take it easy, I am in pain." As we went out the automatic double swinging doors, the driver commented, "I am in pain too. I have not had any lunch and its past three o'clock." I yelled back, "That's not my fault."

Just outside the double swinging doors is a concrete ramp about 30 feet long. It has a vertical drop of about 6 feet. At the head of the ramp, the driver gave the wheel chair a gentle push and let go of the handles. I whizzed down the ramp and into the street. When the wheel chair and I reached the middle of the street, a slow moving Lexus IS F. hit me. The Woman driver was on her cell phone and did not see me. She did not apply her breaks until the collision. The impact threw me onto the pavement; both wheels of the wheelchair were badly bent. Someone called 911 and I was taken to the emergency hospital. More x-rays were taken but I was pronounced OK. I had a few burses and a skin scrape from the rough street pavement. The emergency hospital staff asked if I had a way home. I responded, "I don't want to use the senior citizen's transportation service any more." One of the hospital staff members offered to take me home. I refused because I needed help getting in and out of the car.

The hospital staff was able to arrange for the ambulance to take me home.

When I arrived at my home there was a City police car parked in front of my house. The police officer followed the paramedic helpers and me into my house. After I was comfortable in my big easy chair, the officer gave me a traffic citation. He said that I was driving an unlicensed vehicle on a city street. In addition, that I caused an accident damaging another vehicle. The woman driving the car that hit me wants me to repair the damage to her car. I said, "that is ridicules" and tore he ticket up right in front of the officer.

The officer then left my house. As he was leaving he said, "You are duo in court on Wednesday the third."

I pieced together the torn traffic citation to find the address of the courthouse. I was able to find transportation to the courthouse on Wednesday. You will not believe this Congressman Ferguson but the judge awarded the Lexus IS F driver $800.00 to fix her car. This was the least amount of the three repair estimates produced by the Lexis driver. I also had to pay the court costs. The judge said that if I wanted to drive my wheel chair in the city streets I must purchase license plates for the vehicle. When I saw the story in the newspaper, I learned that the judge was the brother of the Lexis drinker's husband.

"Congressman Ferguson luckily I did not get hurt in the accident. I am out a little over $1,000.00 and I have a broken heart to know that a human can be treated this way. As I said earlier, I do not know if you can help me or not. I guess I do not even know what help I am asking from you. I do want to thank you for hearing my story. If you can have an impact on this kind of injustice, I would be deeply indebted to you."

Congressman Ferguson said, as he wiped away a tear from his eye, "I don't think your situation falls under any of the powers granted to the Federal Government by the Constitution. However, as a loving considerate and passionate human being, I cannot just let your story slide by. I will bring this up with my staff and see what we can do. Thank You Mrs. Lass Paige for a very touching story."

The host asked, "Do we have a question for Congressman Thomas Epstein?"

The barber Host recognized a woman in the third row. She began to speak. "Congressman Epstein, my name is Mrs. Stuckintha Sand; I am a naturalized citizen of the USA borne in Kenya. I married Mr. Hick Sand in 1991 when he was working in Kenya for the United Nations. My question is about the authority given to traffic control police officers. Can a traffic cop pull you over for speeding if you are driving at the normal traffic speed? What I mean by this is if you are in a line of traffic on the freeway and all cars are going 80 miles per hour, can the traffic cop single you out for speeding? The posted speed limit is 65 MPH."

Congressman Epstein answered, "Mrs. Sand, Your question is concerning a local issue. I am your Congressional representative in the United States Congress. I will be glad to hear any concerns you have that are a federal matter, I do not have an opinion on the authority given your local traffic law enforcement people."

The Host said, "Thank you anyway Mrs. Sand."

The barber Host asked for another question. The questioner stood up and announced, "Mr. Congressman Ferguson, I have a problem I believe needs to be addressed by Congress." The Congressman interrupted, "Sir Will you please state your name. My name is Congressman Ernest Ferguson." The man started again, "Congressman Ferguson my name is Abdul Abasheen and I have a problem that needs to be addressed by Congress. It is my belief that new laws need to be written to straighten the meaning and purpose of the first amendment to the Constitution of the United States.

You see Mr. Congressman Ferguson I belong to a little known religious group in southern Louisiana called the ABA-Leens. Our God is ABA We worship ABA. We also worship ABA-Leen which is a very hard rock found on the beaches of our Southern States. ABA-Leen is used to cut marble and garnet. When ABA-Leen is ground up, slurry made from it and goat's milk, a cotton twine is coated with the slurry and drawn across the hard marble, and it cuts the marble like butter.

Mr. Congressman here is my problem. Our religion requires all male worshipers to carry a very sharp 10-inch saber on our belts as a token of being a soldier fighting for ABA. The grand ABBA-Leen Wizard ordered me to the west coast to deliver some church material to the non-believers there. At the airport, I was denied passage because of my religious knife. Mr. Congressman I believe this action on the part of the airport security infringes upon my freedom of religion that is guaranteed in the first amendment to the Continuation of the United States (Bill of Rights).

The First amendment to the Constitution was adopted December 15, 1791 and it gives Freedom of Religion, of speech, of the press, to assemble, and to petition. Mr. Congressman I was denied the right to practice my religion at the airport. I could not deliver the important church papers to the west coast church. The Grand Wizard became furious with me. The grand Wizard told me I would not have a good seat in heaven along with the rest of my fellow worshipers. If this happens, again, I will be thrown out of my church and I will have to turn in my saber. Mr. Congressman Do you see what a mess I am in?" Congressman Ernest Ferguson responded, "Yes, I do see. We make laws from time to time to protect our citizens. If we allowed everybody to carry a sharp 10 knife onto our airplanes we would be courting disaster.

You mentioned the first amendment to the Constitution and it does give freedom of speech. However, you cannot holler, 'FIRE' in a crowded building. Does this violate the meaning of the first amendment? I do not think so. I would like to remind you of an article printed in all of our nationally syndicated newspapers just a week ago. A daughter in a religious family began to date a man in the armed services. The Father felt that this action disgraced and dishonored the family. The father cut his daughter's head off. The father is now serving life in prison. You cannot violate our laws and blame it on your religion. Another case comes to mind. A religious leader sexually assaulted several underage girls. He stated in court that his religion permitted his action. He is now serving a life sentence in prison. No, you cannot violate our civil laws in the name of religion and claim the first amendment as a defense for your action. You need to have a talk with your grand wizard and adjust your religious beliefs. I am sorry Mr. Abdul Abasheen I don't see your problem as something I wish to handle."

"Congressman Ferguson my name is Miss Dorothy Compton. My friends call me 'Dot Com'. I am also affectionately known as a tree hugger. I am an avid ecology 'watchdog'.

My great concern is the current rate of the destruction of our National Forests. We have lumber people taking a controlled number of trees each year. The biggest concern is the 'Forest Fire' problem. We all remember the Yellowstone fire in 1988. That fire destroyed almost 800, 000 acres of timber.

In Arizona, wild forest fires took 975, 000 acres of fine trees in 2005. In 2011, Arizona lost another 982, 000 acres of timber to wild forest fires. I want the Federal Government to rethink its National Forest programs. I would like a two-prong approach to this problem.

First: I would like to sell off 60 feet wide strips of forestland timber that runs from the north border to the south border of each national forest. In addition, I would like to do the same thing going east to west. These strips of treeless land would be made into fire lanes. These fire lanes would enclose a one thousand acre plot of timber. In the center of the fire lane strips of land a 20 foot wide graveled road would be built. Herbicides would be sprayed on the 20 feet road shoulders. This would prevent vegetation growth that would fuel a forest fire. There is nothing sacred about the one thousand acre figure. In the mountainous regions road building may become very expensive. The idea here is to make plots of forest trees that can easily be managed during a wild forest fire. The money from the sale of timber from the 60-foot wide fire lane can go towards the cost of the roads and fire lane.

Second, when the logging people cut down a tree they must replace that tree with two young seedlings of the same species. The two for one program will continue until the forest sciences people determine an effective equilibrium has been reached between our building material needs and the preservation of our National Forests. In any event, the loggers are responsible for the survival of the young seedlings. This means that the logger cannot just throw down a seedling on the ground and walk away. I know this procedure will raise the cost of the lumber that goes unto construction projects. Remember, there is no free lunch. If we are going to preserve our national forests for our grandchildren, we must pay the price. Thank You, representative Ferguson."

Congressman Ferguson responded, "Miss Compton you have some brave ideas on our ecology. I do not know how many people would agree with your enthusiastic approach to the national forest problem but I will run it by my staff. We will then determine if such an approach is possible in the current congress. Thank you Miss Compton."

The host said, "Can we have another question please?"

A woman in the front row stood up to be recognizes. The barber Host told the woman she could speak.

"Congressman Epstein My name is Patricia Christen Turner or PC Turner for short. My friends call me Pan Cake Turner. I would like to see a law passed that would require the large companies that ship jobs overseas to compensate the worker that lost his job. For instance if a USA worker is receiving $20.00 per hour and his job is shipped overseas the compensation should meet the following formula: The company pays the overseas worker $5.00 per hour then the compensation should be $20.00 minus $5.00 or $15.00 per hour. I think this would stop the shipment of our good jobs overseas."

"Thank you Miss Patricia Turner. Your proposal is a very drastic one. I doubt I could get a bill like that trough the house let alone the full congress. I will discuss your suggestion with my staff and maybe we can come up with something."

"Congressman Ferguson my name is Mr. Snow Strum Rainnpour. I am a naturalized citizen of the Unites Stated born in the eastern country of India. I wish you would explain what all of this talk of foreign rate of exchange is all about. It sounds to me like something evil. What say you?" Congressman Ferguson responded, "Well Mr. Rainnpour the answer to your question could easily fill a large book. I will try to answer your question as best I can in the very short time we have left. Let us say that in your country the primary unit of wealth is the 'poly-wigg' much like the dollar is in the USA. A manufacturer in the USA makes a product that sells for 10.00 US dollars each. The USA manufacturer sells his product in your country for $10.00 USA. A rug maker in your country makes a rug that sells for 10 'poly-wigs'. This rug maker sells his rugs in the USA for 10 'poly-wigs' each. When the consumer pays for the merchandise, the selling clerk will accept 10 USA dollars or 10 'poly-wigs in each country. The exchange rate is 1 to 1. Are you with me Mr. Rainnpour?" Mr. Rainnpour said, "I am with you so far."

Congressman Ferguson said, "Great. Your country and the USA both borrow money from the World Bank, right" Mr. Rainnpour said, "yeh, I guess so." Congressional representative Ferguson said, "Well both countries do borrow money from the world bank from time to time. Let us suppose that in country XYZ, you have a severe drought and little or no crops are produced. This is followed by devastating floods. Food, water, oil, and gasoline must be imported into your country to stave off starvation and disease. The need for money to buy the essentials for life is critical. The rug manufacturer needs to sell his rugs in the USA to get money to support his family. He is willing to sell his rugs in the USA for 5 'poly-wigs' each instead of the usual 10 'poly-wigs' each. He also needs to buy the product made in the USA. However, he is only able to pay five 'poly-wigs' each not the customary 10 'poly-wigs' each. The exchange rate is now 2 to 1. The manufacturer in the USA cannot sell his product in country XYZ unless he is willing to accept 5 'poly-wigs' each not the usual 10 'poly-wigs' The poor people in country XYZ cannot afford the American made product because it costs too much. Remember the exchange rate is 2 to 1.

The scenario I just painted for you is rater drastic. In addition, not all exchange rates are this serious. This is a very simplified explanation. I hope this gives you some idea of how the exchange rates work." Mr. Rainnpour said, "Thank you Mr. Congressman. I am just as confused as ever. I will have to think upon it. Thank you very much."

The host asked if there were any questions for congressional representative Ferguson. A young woman raised her hand and she was recognized. My name is Miss Toulouse Plumber and I reside here in the second Congressional district. My problem is with the current home invasion laws. If someone invades your home with the intent to do you harm you are not allowed to shot them. The law says that you must seek any other possible alternative to escape harm. Congressman Ferguson I want home invasion to be rated as a federal felony crime and that you have the right to shot and kill the invader. You see I am the victim of a home invasion. Although I had a loaded .44 magnum revolver in my bed room night stand, I stood by and watched the invader ram sack my home seal my jewelry, take my money from my purse, and sexually molest me. This was six years ago and I still have night mires of that horrible night. The invader was never caught and I am sure he is somewhere enjoying my jewelry and money. We spend too much time trying to protect the civil and human rights of the criminals and do nothing for the victim of the crime. Again Congressman I want home invasion to be rated as a federal felony. The law should give the right to shot and kill the invader to the victim. Thank you for listening to my story." "That was a very touching story Miss Plumber. I seriously doubt that I could get such a bill through Congress but I promise you that I will try."

The Host asked, "Can we have another question please?" A man raised his hand. He was recognized by the barber host. "Congressman Ferguson my name is Stew Driver. I live in a 55-year or older gated community. When my wife and I saw the park's ad in the newspaper, it sounded like an ideal place for us to live. It has a beautiful ballroom, tennis court, pool tables, hobby room, library, swimming pool, and a first class kitchen. When we walked into the sales office, we knew that we had as much power as the park management. We also knew that for a contract to be valid there has to be some exchange of property, material, goods or money from both parties. The park management has a facility that we would like to use. We have money that the park management would like to call their own. We investigated several sources and found that the value of the property was very near the same as the park management's asking price. It seemed like a fair deal to exchange our $120,000.00 for the $120,000.00 home in the park. We moved in without a glitch. We bought new furniture for the living room. We added a new washer and drier to our new home. My wife had to have a new 42-inch TV. We were soon settled down in our new home.

Four months after we signed the contract for our new home, the park management issued a new set of rules and regulations. The new rules state that we cannot have our nice blue flowerpots out in the front yard. The sun-powered or solar lights were also forbidden. The new rules state that the garage door must be fully closed except for entering or leaving in the vehicle. There can be no flagpole in the front yard. The garbage cannot be left on the side of the house. Parking on the street is forbidden unless you obtain a special sticker from the front office.

We took the list of new rules to the park manager and registered a complaint. The park manager said, "You signed an agreement to abide by the park rules." We countered with, "but these were not the rules we agreed to. The Park manager said, "This is my park and I can make and/or change the rules as I please. If you choose not to follow the park rules then you can move out of the park." You see Congressman the park manager has all of the power and we have none. This simply is not right. Two people inter into a contract and suddenly one of the parties to the contract has all of the power. I want to see a federal law passed that will rectify this injustice."

The barber host answered the ringing house phone and quickly announced that the meeting was over.

The Hexagon had just sent a jet plane from DC to Crockersville to pick up Congressman Ferguson and Congressman Epstein. They have to leave immediately as the drive to Crockersville takes a good 45 minutes. It seems that some very long-range missiles were fired from an unfriendly nation. It has not been determined yet what target they will hit. The President wants a quorum in Congress just in case drastic action is needed. He said, "Thank you Ladies and Gentlemen, Good night."

KLAPPTONVILLE-THM

Congressman Paul Nelson was just reviewing the demographic statistics of the last election. He noticed that out of approximately 350,000 registered voters in Klapptonville he received only fifty-three votes although he did carry the third congressional district. He talked to some of his friends that had connections in Klapptonville and asked if they could set up a Town Hall Meeting in the village for him. Sheriff Gottcha Jordon was selected to host the Town Hall Meeting.

Sherriff Jordon brought the meeting to order at the posted time. There were the customary Greetings and introductions before Representative Nelson gave his short sales pitch. At the end of Nelson's little talk, Host Jordon asked for questions from the audience.

Several members had their hand up at the same time. The meeting Host selected the big man in the loud red sweater. The man said, "Congressman Nelson my name is Faugh Horne. My job takes me all over the country. I am at any one location for one year to five years. Rather than rent a house or an apartment, I usually buy a place for wife, my kids, and me. Most of the time I am stuck with a Home Owners Association. They take anywhere from $ 60.00 to $ 120.00 a month out of my paycheck. I attended several of the HOA meetings. I ask, "What am I getting for the $120.00 per month I am paying into the HOA?" The answer that I get goes something like this, "You have security and peace of mind, and we see that the park across the street is mowed. We make sure that no trash is lying around.

We see that all residents follow the rules." I responded, "But the park does not belong to me. I do not care if the park is mowed or not mowed. I mentioned that there are 87 households in this HOA and 87 times $120.00 per month is $10,440 per month or $125,280.00 per year. My house is only worth twice that amount." They come back with, "yes but the park is always mowed. And you can feel secure." "When I left the HOA meeting I stopped by a convince store to buy some milk. The milk was priced at $ 2.85 per gallon. I had just been paying $ 1.49 at a grocery store near my house. I told the clerk this. He said, "But this is blue ribbon milk. See it had a blue ribbon attached to the top. These are pure silk blue ribbons imported from China." I said, "But I don't want any blue ribbons." The clerk said, "Well all of our milk has the blue ribbons." I asked him where he worked before his job at the convince store?" He said, "I used to be the manager of a HOA. "Now Congressman the story is the same everywhere I go. We need some Federal regulations to keep these HOA people in line. They have gone completely bezerk." "The Congressman asked, "Don't you have a remedy for this situation at the polling place? These people are voted into office aren't they?" The man in the red sweater said, "Yes, but they have clicks, buddy-buddy, you know. The same people are voted in every year. If you speak harshly about any of the HOA officers you are chastised by some of your neighbors."

The congressman said, "Sir, I do understand your problem and I do have sympathy for you, but I do not think this is a Federal issue." The man in the red sweater slammed his folded newspaper down on the floor and walked out of the town hall meeting in a huff.

Another man spoke up and said, "Congressman Nelson, my name is Crazy Ed Workin. I lost my job. The market for our little plastic whirly gigs just seemed to evaporate. I and five other employees were laid off because the company could not afford to pay us as no money was conning in from the sales of our whirly gigs. Three months ago, sales picked up again but the manager hired some other workers not the ones that were laid off. We asked why he did not hire us back. "The Manager said, "You guys were making over $20.00 per hour. These new people are working for minimum wage. I just cannot afford you any more, sorry." I said, "Yes, but I am an experienced whirley gig tester and it's expensive to train a guy like me." He said, "You know that training manual you wrote last spring, well it is working out just fine." I said, "Now how can a company lay off experiences workers and hire minimum wage workers to replace them. Can't the Federal Government do something?" The congressman replied, "I'll have to check he facts and see if any Federal Statutes were violated, sir."

Another man with a raised hand was recognized by host Sherriff Jordon. He said, "Congressman Nelson, My name is Reel Tine Louzer. The postal service is part of the Federal; Government, Right? Well my wife ran off with our mail carrier. My neighbors saw them leave in the mail delivery truck. Because the truck is Government property and the mail carrier is a Government employee, I think that the Government is liable for my losses. I had to hire a woman to do my laundry and clean the house. Another woman comes in once a week and cooks me a meal or two. I don't think I am being unreasonable do you?" The rest of the attendees gave out a big laugh. The Representative Nelson responded, "Sir, I think you were negligent in not keeping your wife in toe. She was your responsibility and you neglected your responsibility. You may find that the Federal Government may sue you for spousal neglect. Another big roar came from the attendees. The Congressman Nelson concluded, "No, Sir Mister Louzer, I don't think you have a case here."

A woman was recognized next and she said, "Congressman Nelson, my name is Miss Irene Doolittle or I. Doolittle. I do not think that the Federal Government is doing enough to promote women's rights under the Constitution. The Constitution guarantees us women's rights." The Congressman interrupted by saying, "I am sorry Miss Doolittle, but the Constitution does not address women's rights. In addition, yes I think there is more to be done in this arena. Just what do you have in mind?" She said, "Well I would like to see more women in important positions in the GREY HOUSE DC. I would like to see some women football players. How about some female coal miners? We just do not have a chance in this male dominated society. I want justice. Female justice not male concocted justice." The Representative Nelson said, "Miss Doolittle, your cause is very admirable but it is just not a matter for the Federal Government."

Another Lady spoke up and said, "Congressman Nelson my name is Miss Mercy Kleen Sheets. We have laws against illegal entry into our country. Why cannot the influx of foreigners be stopped? The Congressman replied, "It's like anything else you have to have the will to do it before it gets done. I am a member of Congress, the legislative branch of Government, we do not enforce the laws we only write them. I will carry your sentiments back to THE GREY HOUSE DC.

Congressman Nelson said, "Well thank you all very much for being here tonight. It has been a real pleasure for me to see you all. Please remember your voice is heard at the voting booths. Your vote is very important regardless who your favorite candidate is. Good night and God Bless.

TV TALK SHOW-BUTTER PAYNE

Mr. Butter Payne (Butt Pain) invited several politicians to participate in his "Who's Going to Win" TV Talk Show. Mr. Payne introduced each of the talk show participants in the usual manor. There were three very conservative congressional representatives and three very liberal Congressmen on the panel. There was also a member of a fringe party and an Independent. With eight politicians, all having different views on tonight's subject, this should be a very interesting TV session. Mr. Payne announced, "Tonight's subject is 'How do we fix our sick economy'." Mr. Payne pointed to conservative Congressman Epstein and said, "Why don't you start us off, Sir." Congressman Epstein proclaimed, "Our Economy is not as sick as most people would like to think." Before he could get his last words out, the three liberal Congressman began to chatter, "There is a 8% unemployment rate, In my district there are forty thousand people out of work, The price of gasoline keeps going up." At this point, the three conservative Congressmen all joined in the verbal exchange. Oh, Yes the Independent politician and the fringe party person had their say also. Now with Eight politicians all talking at once Mr. Payne tried to ask another question. Now we have all nine people talking at one time. Is there anybody listening, I think not. What are heard on the voter's TV set are many garbled words. Mr. Payne pounded on the table with his closed fist and announced, "We must break now for a previously tapped soap commercial advertisement." As the Editor/Director of the TV program switched from studio camera "B" to the previously recorded soap commercial you could hear:

"All of my constituents sa . . . . , we have to . . . ., on my side we ha . . . . Leave it alo . . . . , Pass a new la . . . ., Have the government step . . . . , too much government inter . . . . , Private control is th . . . . , Too hard to enforce . . . . , Just watch next Novemb . . . . , My constituents want . . . . , It's impossible to . . . . Loud and clear above the noise: "Just try Slimy-Goo hand and face soap. You will make it your only soap."

The electronic TV listener survey monitors show that 96% of the viewers have switched to another channel on their TV sets. I am sure that each speaker got a lot off his or her chests. I am equally sure that no one listened to a word the panel said.

CHROMOSLIPASIDE

When Senator Kent Miller's wife died, he married his secretary. At that time, he was 59 years old and his new wife was 28 years old. She had just divorced her husband of nine years because he could not support her in the life style that she craved. Senator Kent Miller was able to do so.

During the second year of their marriage Senator Kent Miller developed prostate cancer. The resulting surgery left the Senator erectile deficient. Their marriage seemed to be going well from the outside. At the age of sixty-two the Senator was checking the bank statements and he found an unusual entry on one of the credit card statements It was a $ 49.98 from the Gogetum Drug Emporium. He had never purchased anything from the Gogetum Drug Emporium so he was curious as to what the purchase was about. He called the drug emporium and asked about the credit card entry. The druggist told the Senator that the $49.98 was for Chromoslipaside. The Senator asked the druggist, "What the hell is Chromoslipaside used for?" The druggist responded, "It is a birth control pill. It is a rather fast acting pill. The female takes two pills 20 mg about 10 minutes before intercourse to prevent a pregnancy."

The Senator thanked the druggist and hung up. The Senator did a thorough search through the house and the car but no chromoslipaside could be found. While his 31-year-old wife, Lucille, was taking a shower, the Senator looked through her purse. Sure enough, there was a bottle of chromoslipaside in her purse. The label on the bottle said that it originally contained 30 tablets. The Senator could only count 18 tablets still in the bottle. The prescribing Doctor was a Dr. Alice Smelly Garboon. Dr. Mack Kayvorkin was their regular family Doctor. He replaced the chromoslipaside bottle back into her purse and made a note in his personnel logbook. The Senator's wife, Lucille, belongs to the, "Purple Hat Society" that meets each Friday at 8:00PM. She usually gets home from the meetings around mid-night.

The next Saturday morning while his Wife, Lucille, was in the shower the Senator examined her purse for the bottle of chromoslipaside. Guess what? The bottle contained only 16 tablets of chromoslipaside.

The next Friday the Senator Miller told Lucille he had a business meeting in THE GREY HOUSE DC. Instead of going to THE GREY HOUSE DC he parked in a secluded parking lot one block from the PURPLE HAT SOCIETY's meeting place. Soon his wife arrived at the meeting place. Five minutes later Senator Paul Nelson, a good friend of

Senator Kent Miller arrived at the Purple Hat Meeting place. Senators Kent Miller and Paul Nelson worked together on the federal legalization of medical marijuana bill. Paul did not even get out of the car as Senator Kent Miller's wife, Lucille, came running to meet Senator Nelson. She got into Nelson's car and they drove off. Senator Miller followed them to the FRIENDSHIP MANOR motel just outside of DC. They did not stop at the office but went directly to room 1001A.

Senator Miler drove back home. On his was home he stopped and bought a digital movie camera and a pack of 10 discs. When Lucille came home and had gone to sleep, Senator Miller again counted the number of pills in his wife's purse. There were only 14 pills this time. The next Friday the sane routine occurred except Senator Miller recorded all of the action on his new digital movie camera. After Sunday's lunch, Senator Miller suggested to Lucille that they watch a movie on their big screen TV set. They got real comfortable then the Senator put in the disc of the recorded illicit affair into the TV's DVD player. After a few minutes the Senator exclaimed, "OOPS guess I put in the wrong disc." The Senator said, "Let's count the number of pills in your chromoslipasise bottle that is in your purse." The Senator took the purse from Lucille and counted the pills in front of her.

Well it looks like you have been having a good time, "SISTER." "What do you have to say for yourself, HONEY?" The Senator got on the phone and invited his friend, Senator

Paul Nelson and his wife, over for some food snakes, drinks, and conversation.

When they arrived Senator Miller said, "Here is a little film that I think you both will get a kick out of." He put on the evidence disc. The Senators got into a fistfight and the women got into a hair-pulling contest. The police received a call from a neighbor saying there is a domestic disturbance at the Senator's house. All were arrested and the news media were notified.

The police would not allow interviews in the jail. Both Senators were swamped by reporters when they were released on bail. The story hit the headlines of all the newspapers and was the feature story in several cheap slick cover magazines.

DEAL TOBACCO VS SUBS

Representative Steven Boyd stepped into Representative Kent Miller's office for a little chat. After reminiscing about the good old times, Steven reveled the real purpose of his visit. Steven opened up, "Kent I know you are going to have a hard time getting a tobacco money bill through the house this session. People are just not in favor of giving government money to farmers to raise tobacco when it is known to cause cancer. The voters know darn well that we will turn around and ask for more money for research and development to find a cure for the cancer that the tobacco caused. I know you need all the help you can get. I am in the same boat with you. The Navy has already said that they do not need any more surveillance submarines. The plant in my district is geared up to produce the surveillance subs and I understand that there is a very good profit on each sub. Tell you what I will do. I will put all of my staff to work to help you on your tobacco bill if you will do the same for my submarine bill."

Steven continued, "I am a little embarrassed to participate in the 'I'll rub your back if you rub mine routine."

Kent said, "Steven, you have a deal. Let us have a shot of absolute vodka to seal the deal. Steven said, "You had better make it two shots of absolute vodka. Kent responded, "Sure thing, Steven." A firm handshake and Representative Steven Boyd was on his way back to his apartment.

PAUPERIZE CREAM
Bad Dream

Linda Epstein had just finished her breakfast and was watching her husband Congressman Tom Epstein dunk his donut into his cup of coffee. Just as Congressman Epstein was making his last dunk, Linda asked, "Honey, how did you sleep last night?" Tom responded, "Not too well, I twisted and turned all night long." Linda said, "Yes, I know you woke me up several times with your restlessness. What was the problem?" Tom answered, "Well I had a bad dream. You remember me telling you about Daniel Bachelor telling me that I needed to learn to talk for an hour and not really say anything.?" "Yes, I remember," said Linda. "Do you remember that lobbyist from the Pharmacia Company that took us out to dinner and promised me a brand new Volkswagen beetle? He wanted me to push through congress a bill to reduce the chemical company's tax burden." "Yes, I remember," said Linda. "Well in my dream, I pushed, shoved, cajoled, and bargained until I got his bill through congress. The Pharmacia companies spend lots of money developing and testing new products. The cost to manufacture the product is relative small. The price that the consumer pays for the product is the cost to manufacture plus the cost to develop and test. After seven years when the patent runs out, other manufactures can make the product under the generic name. They can sell the product for less than the brand name product because they do not have the development and testing costs. The Pharmacia Company wanted tax relief on the development and testing cost adds on." Tom continues, "In my dream I got the Volkswagen plus the pharmaceutical company offered me a job in their company.

I had just been promoted to Regional Sales Manager for the Pauperize Cream Division of the Pow Cornerding Chemical Company. We had a regional sales meeting in the Chicago Convention Center that lasted well into the night. I drank quite a bit. All of the meeting members began to chant, Speech... Speech. I reluctantly went to the podium but several big brutes kept pushing me. Oh, my gosh I had to talk about something that I did not know anything about. I began to tell how different people used the pauperize cream. I mentioned how easy it is to ship. In addition, how it almost packs itself. I told them that the jar of pauperize cream did not weigh any more than the empty jar. The retail packaged cream comes with multiple labels and the end user can apply the label most pleasing to them. A pressed wood spatula applicator comes attached to the top of the jar. The glue used to attach the spatula applicator is recyclable. In fact, the glue can be used over and over again. When all of the pauperize cream is used up, the empty jar makes an excellent camping ashtray. At this point, a noisy woman in the audience interrupted me. She wanted to know what the pauperize cream would do to help her. I responded, "Absolutely nothing." I told her that I found a full jar of pauperize cream made an excellent paperweight to hold down my stack of delinquent bills. When asked what was in the pauperize cream I responded by saying that it contained a secret combination of rare snake oils. I said that some of the snake oil used in the cream is more expensive per once than gold. By now, the staff meeting had turned into a regular town hall type meeting.

Another loud elderly woman in the audience stood up and interrupted me by saying, "My name is Mrs. Iona B. Blunt, and I would like to know how Pauperize cream got its name." I said, "That is a very good question and I am glad you asked. Back in the 1930's the marketing staff at POW CORNERDING noted that many of the very poor people had acne. Many of these people could not afford the expensive cortisone compounded creams popularly used to treat acne. This information was presented to top management at POW CORNERDING. The Marketing Department said that there was an untouched waiting market out there. Management issued an order to the Research and Development to come up with a very affordable yet effective treatment for acne. The name," PAUPERIZE CREAM was chosen for the new product. The product was design to help the very poor, the paupers. After a successful development and testing program, Pauperize Cream production began. The night oven operator came to work feeling no pain. After loading the ovens with the Pauperize Cream slurry, he fell asleep. Instead of the specified 45 minute bake time the pauperize cream was cooked for three hours. When the night supervisor realized what had happened, he shut off the oven and woke up the oven operator. After the pauperize cream had cooled the supervisor stuck his index finger on his right hand into the overcooked mess. He wiped off the cream laden right hand index finger on the back of his left hand. After about an hour, he noticed that the warts on his left hand had disappeared.

A closer examination revealed that the skin on his left hand was as smooth as a baby's butt. The supervisor went back to the vat of overcooked pauperize cream and began to apply it all over his body. He reported has findings to upper management. Marketing was elated. It was decided that customers of all financial levels would use this new cream and the name had to be changed from the pauper concept. The new name for the overcooked pauperize cream turned out to be PAPARAZZI CREAM.

The night supervisor wanted to fire the drunken oven operator but management promoted him to General Manager of the PAPARAZZI CREAM Manufacturing operation. Does that answer your question Mrs. Iona B. Blunt?" "Yes, sir it sure does and that was a very interesting story."

I was on a roll so I just kept rattling on, "We have many testimonials declaring the effectiveness of Paparazzi Cream. I have a typical case right here in my hand. This is a case of a 45-year-old mother that received an Electrophysiometry treatment after using Paparazzi Cream for three weeks. The clerk at the convene store refused to sell her beer because she looked under aged.

Her daughter age 16 also uses Paparazzi Cream and after a Phyesocyclometry treatment, she was able to purchase beer for her mother no questions asked.

Due to federal packaging label laws, Paparazzi Cream comes in a brown paper wrapper. The cream is available in three different sizes. The large size weighs a little less than 5 KG, while the medium size weighs approximately 1.0 micro gram. The small size requires special handling and can only be shipped via Pee Wee division (PWD) of China Air Freight (CAF) on weekends.

Here is another customer satisfaction testimonial. As best as we can determine the natives on the island of Bowleen in the Maylackin island chain, contracted a rear disease from the native apes. This disease was passes on to the missionaries from the MultiMate religious group. The missionaries brought the disease back to the United States. The disease, Cardiocrampinitis has no known cure. In a recent breakthrough, it was discovered that a generous application of Paparazzi Cream together with a single treatment of pyrotechnicalslidectomy could inhibit the progression of the disease.

The damaged tissue cannot be repaired, but it appears that Paparazzi Cream is instrumental in preventing further tissue damage.

I think I mentioned earlier that Paparazzi Cream contained some rare snake oils. You might be interested to know that some of these rare snakes can only be hunted by the straight-nosed chicken hawks. The natives train the straight-nosed chicken hawks to hunt the snakes and bring them in to the village for the oil harvest.

At this point, the audience became hostile and began to throw things. The meeting turned into a riot. One old man threw a boiled egg wrapped with a one hundred dollar bill. I kept the hundred bucks and I ate the egg."

LITTLE RED PHONE

The re-election organization party was a great success. All bases are covered and the re-election plan seems to be near perfect. The president did a great job of mingling with the most important people. The President either offered or accepted a drink with about twenty-eight different influential people. He would find out the preferred drink of a party member and he would have a similar drink with that person. A night's mixture of Scotch, Bourbon, Gin Tequila, and Vodka left the President with a sick stomach and a busting headache. The next morning things got worse not better. Tom realizing the President's physical torture called in the President's personal physician. The physician examined the President and gave him something for his hangover. By now, the room was getting a little crowded with eight people. There was the President, The Vice-President, The Physician, The President's Secretary, Tom, The Secretary of Defense, Karen Berkowitz, Eileen Barlow, The Grey House DC Press Secretary, the Senate Majority Leader and the Speaker of the house of Representatives. The Senate Majority Leader took a sip on his martini and set the glass down on the President's desk. The President hollered out, "I wish you would quite pounding on the table. That noise is killing my head." At this point, The Grey House DC Chief knocked on the door with a glass of tomatoes juice for the President. Again, the President said, "Why don't you guys stop pounding on the damn door?" The President noticed his open brief case on his desk that was full of sensitive papers. He stuffed all the papers inside and started towards the large walk-in safe. As he turned from the desk, he fell and landed on top of the brief case and papers went everywhere.

The Senate Majority Leader suggested that the executive power be shifted from the President to the Vice-President as the President is in no position to execute his ditties. The Physician has to make this decision replied Karen Berkowitz the secretary of defense. The telephone began to ring in one contentious ring. The President said, "Turn that damn thing off, the noise is killing me." "We cannot, Mr. President, that is the little red phone from MOSBULL in CRUSHOE. It cannot be shut off, replied Karen. Tom nervously picked up the little red phone and said, "Hello, This is The Grey House DC may I ask who's calling, Please?" There was a moment of silenced them Tom heard, " . . . Ahaaaaa . . . . Ahaa We are very sorry sir but there has been a little mistake here ahaa ahaaa. When our radar surveillance detected your practice launce of three unarmed missiles from your Hawaii missile site this information was transmitted, in a scrambled code, to our intelligence in The CRIMELAND. The situation was quickly evaluated and the following message was sent to our missile operating people." At this point Tom put the phone conversation on the loud speaker. "Do not fire the level two missile battery. During the code scrambling the "Do not" was not transmitted to our missile people. All they heard was, "Fire the level two missile battery." As a result they fired three nuclear-armed missiles with a major east coast city address as a target in your country also two nuclear armed missiles were fired with your capitol city address as a target. We are very sorry for this little mistake. We have our entire missile Engineers staff working on this little problem.

If we can, we will destroy the nuclear-armed missiles somewhere over the Atlantic ocean we will do so. If we cannot do that, we will try to divert the nuclear-armed missiles to other targets over the Atlantic. Again, Sir we are very sorry for this little mistake. Please be advised that this was a mistake but if you choose to retaliate by sending missiles our way, we shall unleash all of our nuclear armed missiles and wipe you off the mad. Again we are sorry for any incontinence that we may have caused you." Click and they hung up.

The President said, "Karen, please call the Commander of our of our nuclear missile defense arsenal and tell him that the President and Commander-in-Chief of the Armed Forces has ordered a stand-by alert. Those people are not going to get away with this. Doc. gives me another pill for this busting headache and something for my blood shot eyes. As commander in chief of the armed foresees I am calling for an all-out strike against any aggressor that invades our soil by land, sea, or air." The Senate majority leader said, "Doctor you must declare this man out of his mind and shift the executive power to the Vice-President." The Doctor took the President's blood pressure and said, Oh my God call 911 this person is going to the hospital. The Senate majority leader said, "Vice-President it is all yours and good luck."

The President spent the rest of the day and that night and part of the next day in the army hospital.

When he returned, he resumed his duties as President and Commander-in-Chief of the armed Forces.

One of the first questions he asked was, "Call the Secretary of Defense and find out what happened to those MOSBULL nuclear missiles?" The secretary of Defense informed the President that MOSBULL military was able to destroy the missiles over the Atlantic long before they could reach us.

AIR FORCE ONE-KENT MILLER

"Say Mr. President, the party is going great. Everybody seems to be really enjoying themselves I know I am having a ball, This is a great place to just set and relax," said House Representative Kent Miller. The President responded, "You are right Congressman. We need more of these kinds of parties around here." The congressional representative Miller came back with, "Speaking of relaxing I am in the need of some R and R. I have not spent any time with my wife and kids since the Presidential election. I have been working my butt off, if you will pardon the expression." The President said, "I know what you mean Congressman I have the same feeling." Congressman Miller said, "You know Mr. President, you owe me a favor for all of those farm votes, I pulled in for you. My wife is bugging me to take a vacation in Hawaii. I did a little snooping and I found out that AIR FORCE 1 is not scheduled for a trip this month and besides you have two identical 747 decoys that are idle right now. How's about letting me and the family fly to Hawaii for a little fun in the sun, huh pall. I know you let Senator Chiseler and his family fly to Europe last month on Air Force 1. I promise to return the plane in good shape." The President responded, "There will be a full colonel in charge he will see that it gets back OK."

The President added, "We'll check with Eileen Barlow the secretary of defense and if your information is correct you will be on a plane bound for Hawaii." "Good job Mr. President," said Congressman Miller.

FREELANCE LOBBYST CLAUDE HAMMER

Exactly one month after their last encounter Congressman Kent Miller and Congressman Steven Boyd were setting at the bar when they saw Claude Hammer approaching. Steven spoke up in addition, said, "Hi Claude, who are you lobbying for today?" Claude responded, "Glad you asked, I have a new client that you may find very interesting. Three-research scientist broke away from an old established medical drug manufacturing concern and formed their own limited liability company. These people all have PHD degrees from Placid Medical School at the Oxnard University on the west coast. The name of their new company is, 'Abbit, Cabbit, and Rabbit Medical Research Company, LLC.' Each of these people is an excellent salesperson. They talked to their co harts and sold them an interest in their company. They rose over six million in less than a week. I have 5 million of their money in my checking account for expenses on this lobbying effort.

Now I am going to tell their story just like it was told to me. They said, "When you walk down a path and stump your toe, it hurts, Right? Well there is no intelligence in your big toe to tell you not to do it again or to watch out for the big rock or how bad the hurt really is. The nerve endings on the big toe send an electrical impulse up the nerve channel to the brain where all evaluations and decisions are made. The part of the brain that receives the electrical impulse is called the INTERPRETER. The interpreter must take the impulse trigger and develop a scenario that the main part of the brain can use. In order to develop this scenario the interpreter utilizes another part of the brain called the. COMPARATOR. The comparator searches all of the brains memory to find a similar set of conditions to the current set.

All of our experiences are recorded somewhere in the brain's memory and the things that we learned from these experiences are also recorded. The comparator finds the best match and presents it to the interpreter. The interpreter passes along a good scenario the main part of the brain where decisions are made. We now have on the market drugs that can modify the links between the comparator, the interpreter and the maim part of the brain. For example, the brain receives a signal that there is a level eight pain on a scale of one to ten. These drugs can change the pain level from eight to a three. These drugs are commonly referred to as 'pain killers.' The three scientists were successful in changing a good tasting food into a bad tasting food. On three separate experiments, ice cream was made to taste bad and the patient spit it out. These were no hypnosis used in the experiments.

These three people want the federal government to issue grant money for further research into this medical field. They want 20 subs stations of researchers to each work on a small portion of the problem. Of course, Abbit, Cabbit and Rabbit Medical Research Company, LLC would supervise the whole plan. My job is to get some legislators on board and tack on a rider to a sure thing bill to provide the grant money. Just think gentlemen, a drug that can make bad things taste good and good things that taste bad. It would be possible to lose an arm or leg without any pain. In fact, severe trauma could be made to feel good. Well I am going to let you fellows think about it. There is a fortune to be made right here if we play our cards right.

All of my dealings with the firm have been through Mr. Rabbit. His first name is Jack. I will tell Jack that I talked to you two.

I will talk to you later. Have a good day people." Claude left in a hurry. while Steven and Kent were scratching their heads.

PREPERATION FOR REELECTION CAMPAIGN

Mr. Wineseller said, "Mr. President you are being accused of offering nothing and opposing everything on the raising the national debt issue. You are going to have to make some proposals whether or not they have any chance of making it through congress. One more piece of advice I want to give you Mr. President, "When a crisis arises you must maneuver to put the crisis on your side. If there is no crisis, you must create one. This campaign is going to be a very tough one. It's a dog eat dog world out there and if you are going to play the game you are going to get dirty.

The opposition is claiming that you made promises that you did not keep. Do not respond to these accusations. All politicians make promises that they cannot keep. This is politics. If you are asked about a specific promise, say that you do not make the laws. Congress makes the laws. Congress simply did not follow your suggestions, requests, or recommendations. Our fund raising effort is not paying off as it did four years ago. Some of the old time contributors say that they will not ride a losing horse. The polls show you are running behind the opposition. If the election were held today, you would lose by a 30 to 70 % margin. We have raised less than 30 % of the money we raises last election. Mr. President we are going to lose this election unless the opposition makes a very foolish mistake. If you do win, it will be because of the opposition's mistakes not any action on your part. Mr. President I will do everything I can to help you but it looks hopeless. Mr. President let us try something different. Let us do town hall meeting much like the ones that the Congressmen uses. We will try it out in a small town as a test run. The President said, "OK, let's give it a try." Orders were given to the Campaign Manager set up a town Hall Meeting in a small town called Death Valley Dooms. The local party chief politician was appointed host for the meeting. The Host Mr. Henkins Jenkins made the customary preliminary staff prepared speech before introducing the President.

The Introduction went something like this, "I am sure our featured guest needs no introduction, so here is The President of The United States of America. Mr. President." The President gave a talk from the pages of his speechwriter's work. At the end of the President's talk the host Mr. Henkins Jenkins asked if there were any questions from the audience." An elderly Man raised his hand and Mr. Henkins Jenkins said, "You may speak sir." The man said, "Mr. President my name is Mr. Hank Crank. My friends call me Hand Crank. I have paid into Social Security ever since I was 16 years old. I retired at age 70. I know that you did not write the law changing Social Security Benefits but you did sign the bill. I voted for you four years ago, but I am having serious doubts this time. Do you intend to take away everything from us older voters?"

The President responded, "Thank you Mr. Hank Crank for your vote four years ago. Let me see what I can do to get your vote this election. First of all Mr. Hank Crank I had to sign the Social Security Bill as it was attached to the legal debt limit legislation. No, Mr. Hank Crank I am not in favor of reducing the Social Security benefits of you older citizens. If I am reelected, I will push members of my party to repeal that bad law. Does that satisfy your justifiable concern?" Mr. Hank Crank said, "Yes Mr. President it certainly does." Host Henkins Jenkins asked for another question. A young Lady in the front row raised her hand. Host Jenkins pointed at her and said, "You may speak." She stood up and said, "Mr. President my name is Miss Havinga Ball. You have several women in your Cabinet and on your administrative staff at the present time; do you plan to have a more women on your team if elected next term?" The President responded, "Miss Havinga I will choose the most talented and personable team mates I can find whether male or female." Host Henkins Jenkins asked for another question.

A man on the front row raised his hand and he was recognized by host Jenkins. He said, "Mr. President my name is Mr. Swimin Poole. Our Country is in a bad fix for money. We must raise the borrowing limit in order to pay all of our government bills. Please tell me why in the dickens are we sending our money to Africana, Parkesburg, South Americana, and the Far East? The President responded, "Mr. Swimin Poole I certainly see your concern and I will look into it as soon as I get back to DC." Host Jenkins asked for another question.

A young woman in the center of the auditorium raised her hand and was recognizes by host Jenkins. In a very strong voice she said, "Mr. President my name is Miss Ugodda Stirwell. I want to know what our country is coming too. A Plaque containing the Ten Commandments had to be removed from in front of a South Carolina Court House because it mixed religion with government. There are no more prayers in our schools. Mr. President I was raised on family prayers." The President interrupted Miss Stirwell, "Young Lady the prayers in school are forbidden by our Constitution." Miss Stirwell Interrupted the President, "When I was in Elementary school we had prayer every morning." The President said, "yes, but that is against the Constitution. Miss Stirwell." "Don't gives me that malarkey we had the same Constitution then as we do now. You people have put a spin on the meaning of the Constitution and I do not like it." A big roar of applause came from the audience as Miss Stirwell spoke. "The first amendment to the Constitution gives us all freedom of speech. I have to be very careful of what I say. The words I use may offend somebody. You and your buddies up there in DC quote the First Amendment when it is to your favor but you just turn your head when it is not in your favor. Another thing we treat our convicted criminals as if they were royalty because of the fear of reprisals from the civil rights groups. There is no mercy for the victims of crime but plenty for the convicted criminals. Mr. President these complaints are wrong and you know it. I have not seen anything on your part to fix it.

A criminal comes into a home and beats an elderly couple to death. You must be very careful not to violate the criminal's civil rights. When I was a child, convicted criminals were put on chain gangs and they busted rocks, today they have big screen HD television in each room and catered room service. Now you tell me that is right. One thing I have noted about you Mr. President You stick by the laws that you like but you fail to enforce the laws you do not like. For example, Border Security." Another big round of applause comes from the listening audience. Miss Ugodda Stirwell took her seat. Host Jenkins asked the Sergeant-at-Arms to remove Miss Ugodda Stirwell from the auditorium for being unduly disrespectful of the President of The United States. The Host Jenkins immediately asked for another question before the President could respond to Miss Stirwell.

A young Man was recognized in the back of the room. He said, "Mr. President My name is Mr. Popsee Cicle, My friends call me POPCICLE. I am 19 years old. I have paid into Social Security for three years now. You signed a bill to adjust the beginning of Social Security benefits to begin at age 70. The Insurance Longevity charts show the average age of the American Male to be 80 years. According to your new plan, I will pay into Social Security until I am 70 years old (54 years). If I have an average life expectancy, I will receive benefits for 10 years. If I fall into the 2-sigma population group, I will receive Benefits for only four years or less. Now I ask you Mr. President does this sound like the right thing to do? I pay for 54 years and receive benefits for only four years."

The President responded by saying, "Mr. Cicle I have no control over your life expectancy. It is possible that you will live to be 100. Then you could collect Social Security Benefits for Thirty years." At this point, the audience began to boo the President and would not quiet down at the host's pleading.

Later Presidential Political Advisor Wineseller said to the President, "Looks like the Town Hall Meeting thing is out."

New Campaign Management Team

After the Death Valley Dooms Town Hall Meeting, Damon Wineseller paid a visit to the 'Last Chance Motel' Presidential suite. The Last Chance Motel is the only motel in Death Valley Dooms. The President offered Damon a drink and the two seated themselves comfortably around a small conference table. Mr. Wineseller spoke first, "Well we have tried the Town Hall Meeting routine and it doesn't seem to pay-off. We do not have the money for a campaign like four years ago. As of to date we have collected less than 30% of the money raised four years ago. I personally do not know what to do. The poles after each speech do not show any excitement for your reelection.

The President spoke, "Mr. Wineseller get a hold of my secretary, Thomas Zachariah, and have him set up a meeting in the round office conference room. I want the Campaign Manager, all of my cabinet members, and The Grey House DC Press Secretary to attend the meeting. We are going to make some changes.

The President and his entourage arrived back at The GREY HOUSE DC at 10:00AM. The reorganization meeting was set for 3:00 PM. The President began the meeting by asking the Campaign Manager to stand up please. The President said, "Things are not going good at all. I am going to make some changes to see if we can get this thing turned around. Miss Eileen Barlow will you stand up please?" Miss Eileen Barlow, Press Secretary, you are fired. You may leave the meeting now. Mr. Campaign Manager you are fired. Please take your speechwriters with you. You may leave the meeting now.

The President continued," Will Miss Nuddy Dancer stand up please. Miss Dancer you are the new Campaign Manager as of this moment. There are seven potential speechwriters waiting for you in the outer lobby, please start your interviews as soon as we leave this meeting."

Miss Nuddy Dancer has five years' experience as CEO of a chain of ten fashionable boutique stores. Before that, she managed packaging of raw hog sausage for three years. She attended the University of Konuchia in the Philippines. She majored in comedy script writing. She wrote the TV script for the 'Dead man returned' series. She also has experience as a foreign money exchange officer in a small bank in South Africa. She owned and operated a septic tank sewer cleaning business and gourmet café in Corruptville for three years.

The President continued," I want everyone to welcome Miss Nuddy Dancer and wish her well in her new job as Presidential Campaign Manager. Tom please set up a meeting tomorrow include everyone here except the old campaign manager, old Press Secretary, and old speechwriters. Invite anyone else you think should attend. We will map out a new strategy to win the upcoming election. Miss Nuddy Dancer I want a plan on my desk by 9:00 AM showing your thoughts on our new campaign strategy. You may use the services of THE GREY HOUSE DC Personnel and Employment Department to fill out your staff. That is all. The meeting is adjourned."

The next day the President called his re organization meeting to order at 2:00PM. The President spoke, "I see we have a new Presidential Campaign Manager, A new Press Secretary, and four new speech writers. The purpose of this meeting is to develop a new plan for my re election in November. I have a suggested outline of a new plan from Miss Nuddy Dancer our new Presidential Campaign Manager.

First, let me say we have tried the Town Hall meeting thing without much positive results. Mr. Damon Wineseller and I have agreed that Town Hall Meetings are out. We do not have enough money to do a first class Campaign like the one we did four years ago. What we do from here on out must be cost effective. We need to set up a measuring scheme that will give us a dollar per vote figure. Can you handle that Miss Dancer?" She responded, "Yes Sir, Mr. President." The President continued, "We have to watch our pennies, you know. In the past, we have not taken advantage of the radio and TV news releases that we could have. Hand pass-outs are cheap. Signs on the City street corners and in voter yards are not that expensive. The biggest thing that Miss Nuddy Dancer has suggested in her brief outline is the telephone calls from supportive voters. Man, those calls are cheap. Miss Dancer, I want you to get with some software people and develop an automated call system to remind voters of the Election Day and put in a plug for me. The software may cost a bundle but we will get thousands of free calls. Sounds like a good idea, Miss Dancer. In addition, Miss Dancer has suggested that we set up a buddy system in the call center where the listening voter is transferred to another supporter for a sales pitch. We need to put out a newsletter and tell our supporters haw to approach other voters and gently slip in the sales pitch. We will have a follow up meeting tomorrow and every day for the next ten days. The meetings will be held in the round office. The meetings will be at the same time unless otherwise advised. If you should come up with another bright idea to win the election, please contact Miss Nuddy Dancer. Ok people we have a lot of work to do so let us get at it. That is all. The meeting is adjourned."

The Big Plot

Damon Wineseller dialed the President's private telephone number from Thomas Vincent Zachariah's office. When the President answered his private phone, Damon announced, "Damon Wineseller here. I need to see you now it is urgent." The President said, "Sure Damon come on in." Damon seated himself in one of the plush easy chairs at the side of the President's desk. Damon started the conversation, "As you know most of our big money contributors have abandoned us. The support among some of our most ardent backers is withering away. Voters are in a fiercely anti-incumbent mood. We have to do something and do it fast. As it stands right now, there is nothing we can do to insure positive results in the coming November Presidential Election. If we win in November, it will be because of a mistake on the part of the opposition, a Big Mistake. We can try to ride out the storm or become proactive. I know what I am about to purpose goes against your grain. I might add against my ethics also. Do you remember that lobbyist Early Knapp? He has been known to do some shady deals. In fact, some of his dealings have been on the edge of what we call ethical practices." The President interrupted, "Don't get my name mixed up in any shady deals, Damon." Damon replied, "Absolutely not Mr. President. I would like to hire lobbyist Early Knapp and see if there is anything in our opponent's past that we could use to our advantage. If lobbyist Early Knapp cannot find something we can use then create a situation that will turn the voters away. I know this sounds drastic but if we are to win in November, we must do something drastic." The President responded to Damon, "I don't want to do this but I don't want to lose in November."

The President pressed '07' on his desk communicator and told Thomas Vincent Zachariah to set up a meeting tomorrow in the circular office of THE GREY HOUSE DC. This will be a secrete closed door meeting between lobbyist Early Knapp, yourself, Damon, and me." Tom was able to contact lobbyist Early Knapp after several tries. Lobbyist Early Knapp was eager to meet with the President and accepted the invitation no questions asked.

The unadvertised meeting took place in the circular office of THE GREY HOUSE DC at 10:00 AM the following day. Damon Wineseller presided over this secret meeting.

Damon summarized the problem for lobbyist Early Knapp's benefit. He expressed the gravity of the situation and the need for immediate action. Damon explained that a politically unknown person had entered the Presidential race with a pocket full of cash. As of this meeting, this person has a war chest three times that of the President.

Damon turned to lobbyist Early Knapp and said, "We want you to dig up some dirt on this new Presidential candidate. If you cannot find a significant piece of dirt then create a situation. If you are successful, it will mean $100,000.00 in your pocket tax-free. Lobbyist Early Knapp said, "I have been working with a call girl on another case that might be interested. Maybe I can get her to claim a rape case against this person that is giving you a problem. The detectives probably will want DNA samples as proof of the claim. Maybe we should just settle for a claim of sexual harassment. I am sure she would go for that. This will cost you extra $10,000.00 cash for the call girl."

Damon reiterated, "The President's name must never be mentioned in this plot in any way shape or form." Lobbyist Early Knapp said, "I understand perfectly. This operation will be strictly between me and the call girl, no one else." Damon announced, "There is $100,000.00 in cash in the Presidents safe. It has your name on it. We all wish you the best of luck. It goes without saying this meeting never did occur, Right?" Damon concluded the meeting with a round of handshakes.

Bulla Kiniginghouse-Contributer

Bulla Klinginghouse is a 76-year-old widow. She owns 17% of a holding company that in turns owns 40% of a large distilling facility. She is wealthy beyond belief. In the last hour and one half, Bulla had downed five double shots of very dry Tanqueray martinis. Bulla was feeling no pain. When she spotted Congressman Greg Biggs, she rushed over to greet him. She said, "Remember me, Congressman Biggs. I made a generous contribution to your election campaign after you made that wonderful speech at the County Community College two years ago?" Congressman said, "Oh yes, I remember you. (Congressman could not remember her name but he did recognize her face) How have you been?" She said, "Oh, ok for an old fat." Bulla then said, "you know, Congressman, you owe me a dance." Greg took another sip of his scotch and water. Bulla said, "Congress man, put that damn drink down and put your arms around this fat lady and let's dance." Greg glided across the floor with bulla stepping on his feet constantly. About half way through the dance number, Bulla said, "Greg, have you ever had an itch where you couldn't scratch it?" Greg said, "Yes, I guess so." Bulla said, "I have one right now and it's driving me crazy. It is on my back right under my brassiere strap hook. Wonder if we could go into one of the side chambers and you could run your hand up under my blouse in the back and scratch it for me?" Well now, this was one of the major contributors to his election campaigns, I cannot say no. Greg replied, "Sure I can handle that." They danced over towards one of the side chambers and entered the room. The lights were out but a flick of the switch fixed that. Greg slipped his hand up under the back of Bulla's blouse and began to scratch with his fingertips.

Bulla said, "No, Greg use your finger nails and scratch hard. Its right under the hook on my brassiere strap. Un hook my brassiere strap." Greg had a difficult time un-hooking her brassiere as it was tight around her body as it was holding up a large amount of real estate. Bulla said to Greg, "Come on around the side with your finger nails." Greg then said, "Well Bulla that is the medical treatment for the day." As they left the room Greg worked the latch on the door to unlock it but it was already unlocked. He was certain that he had locked the door latch when they first came in. Sure enough, the door latch was broken and would not lock. Bulla went to the bar in addition, ordered another dry martini. Greg looked around for a more suitable dance partner. Guess what?" Greg hooked up with one of Hammond's old friends Eileen Barlow the former Presidents Press Secretary. Now Eileen was nothing like Bulla. Eileen was a great dancer and with a shape that would make a dead man come up out of his grave. She was 5 feet 6 inches tall and weighed a mere 125 pound. She has long black hair that stood out against her white evening dress. Her dress was very open in the back and Greg enjoyed the feel of her soft warm skin. While dancing with this lovely woman, Greg felt a gentle tap, tap on his shoulder. It was another one of his campaign contributors wanting to break in and dance. Greg said to himself, "DAMN." That is the custom at these kinds of parties. You can break in on another couple and dance with whom you please. This woman was a better dancer than Bulla, But not as good as Eileen was. Well this woman knew about the side chambers also. Now Greg was not a bad looking fellow and as these women consumed more and more alcohol Greg looked even better. Soon the dance partner started complaining about her feet hurting. She said, "If you were a great gentleman and offered to rub my sore feet, I would not refuse you. You know they really do hurt and you have such big strong hands. What do you say Congressman? We are right next to a side chamber and nobody will see us go in. What you say, Greg?" Greg danced her right up to the door of the side chamber. He opened the door and they went in. She sat on the straight wooden chair and pulled her evening dress up well past her knees. Her legs were well shaped with no hair or varicose veins. In fact, her legs were as smooth as a baby's butt. She placed one of her feet on Greg's lap. Greg began to rub first one foot then the other, She requested, "Go on up to my calf's, they hurt too. Do you like my legs?" Greg said," Your legs are very nice, soft, and smooth."

Greg began to think, I wander if this is really worth it. Greg said, "You know we really better quite before things get out of hand. She said, "yes, you are right I am beginning to feel myself starting to float. She rearranged her clothes and they left the side chamber.

THE GREY HOUSE DC
POLITICS-REP-STRAWBIRD

Senator Berry Barr rushed up to Congressman Biggs just outside of the Congressional Cafeteria and exclaimed, "Congressman Biggs I need your help." This was the introduction that Congressman Greg Biggs received front Senator Berry Barr. The Senator continued by saying, "You know that you owe me a favor for the reforestation effort I gave you last fall" He continued, "I am in deep trouble. You have a member of your finance committee from my state that wants my Senate seat so bad he can taste it. Everything that guy touches turns into gold." Representative Biggs interrupted, "Hold on Senator, just who you are talking about?" Senator Berry Barr responded, "That tall blond Rep. Strawbird, of course. We have to do something to tarnish his good old boy image. If you know of a proposition that is going to fail, we need to get him hooked up to it. I am going to write a bill and attach his mane to it near the back of the bill. I am going to suggest they we tax all of the old woman widows and send the money to hookers in Carmanghea Poe. No body reads these damn bills anyway. I will have to get on the floor and point out the wording just before the vote. I do not know what is wrong with this person; he turned down an opportunity to sleep with one of Hammond Bacon's beauties. I had a research group do study on him. They found that his high school IQ was only 98. He is almost stupid. His record is as clean as a whistle. I have been elected and reelected to two terms in the Senate and I am lot about to give up this job. That person has to be stopped. He simply does not know how to play the political game. I know that you as the Chairman of the Faineance committee can help me destroy this person.

Right now, his record is clean but I know you can mess it up. I am willing to do anything to stop this Guy. Congressman P.P. Baylor has tentatively committed himself to a yes vote on the Federal Medical Adjustment issue. Just before the closing arguments and discussions on the Federal Medical Adjustments bill the speaker of the house took an unofficial poll of the floor and found that the Congressmen were equally divided on this issue. This makes Congressmen Baylor and Strawbird's vote very critical. Their votes are normally called swing votes as they can swing the outcome of the voting either way. Lobbyist Claude Hammer offered to buy Baylor and Strawbird a new mustang GT each for a positive vote on the impending bill before the House. He also offered to buy their wife's a similar car if the bill passed. Congressman Baylor took Claude Hammond up on the bribe. Congressman Strawbird rejected Claude Hammer's offer.

Three weeks later Strawbird had to buy his wife a new car as hers went sour. I just do not understand this guy. He is just plain crazy. He is living in a different world. We simply do not need a guy like that in the Senate. He is bad for my State and bad for the country. Image a person like that making laws that affects all of us. He just does not see the forest for the trees. If everybody in Congress were like him, our nation would be in one hell of a mess. I need your help to stop this person. This person is something else. I hear that he refused a night out with one of Hammon Bacon's blond beauties."

LOBBYIST HAMMON BACON

Hammon Bacon is a very successful registered lobbyist for the Arms and Liquor industry. His position is that there is too much federal regulation in his field of interest. He figures that if he can get the President on his side, He and the President could persuade Congress to lighten up on the regulations. Lobbyist Hammon Bacon personally financed a drinking party at THE GREY HOUSE DC. The purpose of the party was to aid his alcohol producing clients. Prior to the party he paid a private visit to the President's Office. During the visit, the President took Hammon on a tour of THE GREY HOUSE DC. After visiting the large gourmet kitchen, the President showed Hammond the wine cellar.

Hammon noticed that there was very little good tequila in the wine cellar. Hammon said to the President, "Looks like you got room for a few cases of 'CABO WABO' tequila." Hammon pulled out his cell phone and told his waiting truck driver to bring in twenty cases of 'CABO WABO' tequila. The President said, "I'll have to give clearance to the guard for the truck to enter the back delivery gate." One phone call from the President was all it took and twenty cases of

CABO WABO tequila were setting on the wine cellar floor. Hammon said, "I hope to see lots of Margaritas at the party tonight." The President responded, "Well it won't be because we don't have enough tequila, Right." Hammon commented, "You know it looks like you could use some good imported beer." Another quick phone call and the beer was in place in the wine cellar. Hammon asked the President if he was sure he had enough, 'Black Forest' ham for the party. The President said "We will have to check with the Chief on the way out" Three cases of the very best black forest ham was delivered before the party started.

The President commented, "Well it looks like we are all set for one hell of a party tonight."

Hammon thanked the President for the private tour and left. Hammon Bacon had influence with several good-looking young party girls in addition to the ones that worked for him full time. He contacted two of the best looking ones and invited them to the Hammon Bacon sponsored President's party. Hammon instructed the girls to complain about the restrictions placed on the liquor industry. He wanted them to pay particular attention to the underage drinking laws. He would like to see 16 year olds be able to buy liquor legally. He told the girls to, "Dance with the Senators and Congressmen and to be sure that the men always had a drink in hand. If you see a Senator without a drink, go and get him one. If the drink is not his favorite drink, just pour it out and get his favorite drink. He said, "Keep the ball rolling, right girls."

Hammon took the two girls to a fashionable boutique and bought them some very expensive low cut in the front evening dresses, black hose, and black high heel shoes. He told the girls, "I expect to make some real progress tonight for my clients. I expect you to turn on all your charm. If we are successful I will make worth your time." Having said that, Hammon Bacon left for his hotel to dress for the party of all parties.

Hammon picked up the two girls at 7:00 PM. The three of them arrived at THE GREY HOUSE DC at 7:50 PM, 10 minutes before the band starts playing at 8:00 PM. Hammon walked into the hall with two girls one on each arm.

Hammon wore a two-piece brown suit, Brown shoes and socks, a light brown shirt and a dark brown necktie. The two girls were dressed in their new black low cut evening dresses with black shoes and black hose. Each carried a small Black Hand bag. Both girls had beautiful long blond hair. One was 5 feet 8 inches tall while the other one was 5 feet 9 inches tall. All eyes were glued upon the threesome as they paraded down the aisle towards the bar. When they reached the bar they did an about face and started back when the headwaiter stopped them and asked if they would like a table near the band? Hammon replied, "No, We would like to set next to the isle that leads up to the band." They were comfortably seated and the band started playing. Each girl spotted a Senator and asked if they would like to dance. It was hard to refuse such a lovely woman in a black evening dress with only a thin strap on the backside. It was so easy to grab a hold of a hunk of warm soft skin as you danced around the floor. It took only five or six steps before the Senator was asked how he stood on teenaged drinking. The Senator responded by saying, "It's illegal for a teenager to buy and drink alcoholic beverages" The Blond continued, "You know that if a 16 year old girl wanted to drink she could find a way to do so." The Senator said, "But you know that a 16 year old girl should not be able to buy liquor. That is what the law says." She said, "When I was 15years old I had to get someone to buy it for me. I had a boy friend that was 21 years old and he would buy me liter of Scotch every week but he would want me to give him a BJ. I was always afraid that I would get some sort of a disease from him as he had several other girlfriends." Before the Senator could respond, the dance ended and they parted ways.

The two blond girls re-joined company and started towards the table when they noticed two young women standing all alone just where they were before the dance started. The blonde-haired people walked over and introduced themselves. When asked, "Why aren't you girls dancing?" The response was, "We don't know anybody here and besides no one has asked us to dance." The blonds said, "Come on let us introduce you to our boss, he is such a nice guy and he can introduce you to some Senators and Congressmen." The two blonde-haired people introduced the two young women to their boss. It is not right for nice looking young women not to dance. His name is Hammon Bacon but we call him Ham and Bacon. Very shortly, the band started up again and the blonds searched for another target. They spotted two men walking away from the bar. They positioned themselves right in their path and said, "I sure would like to dance this number." The two men grabbed a blond each and away they went dancing the waltz. The two men were Congressman Norman Christopher and Congressman Greg Biggs. The Congressmen each grabbed a hold of a hand full of flesh and smiled happily. It was not long before the routine began about the teenage drinking. "Do you think that a 16 year old girl should be able to buy alcoholic beverages?" asked one of the blonde-haired people. The Rep. responded, "I don't know, why you ask?" "Well when I was 16 I used to drink a little but I had to get an older person to buy it for me. Just about every time they would ask for favors from me. Many of the people did not like to use protection and I was always afraid I would get a disease. However, if you want it bad enough you will do anything, you know what I mean? What your stupid law does is to force young girls run risks that may ruin their lives. However, you do not need to worry I do not have a disease."

After the dance number, the two blonds and Hammon Bacon re-grouped at the table. Hammon commented to the girls, "I am a little worried. The people are not drinking as much as they should for a shindig like this." At 11:00 PM, the party had been going for three hours and the rich old women began to pour in. Most of these girls knew good liquor when they saw it. They ordered only the top shelf stuff. The GREY HOUSE DC auditorium had several small rooms on the side that were designed for people to remove their snowshoes during bad weather. These rooms had one straight back wooden chair, one easy chair recliner, and one small couch. Some of the rich old women would like to take their drinks into one of these small rooms and enjoy the peace and quiet to sooth their nerves, and engage in a little private gossip. One of the blonds noticed a couple of old women leaving one of the rooms and thought to herself that there were some possibilities there.

The next dance one of the blonds asked Congressman Daniel Bachelor to dance and of course, he accepted the invitation. She was very good at the underage drinking routine by now. The blond said, "The stupid underage drinking restriction was doing more harm than good. Teenagers can get liquor with ease. Teen-age girls have to pay a very dear price for their liquor, as the boys usually want sex of some kind in return for the liquor favor. Most of the boys want to exchange a bottle of liquor for a BJ. When they prefer straight sex they do not use protection many of the guys have several sex partners and the chance of being infected is very great. Therefore, your teenage drinking is promoting the spread of sex related disease. I have never had a venereal disease so you do not have to worry about me, Daniel," I wish we could go into one of those little side rooms so I can talk to you more about my concern about teenage drinking restrictions. You think we can do that?" Daniel said, "Sure, there is no harm in talking, Right." When the current dance number ended they entered one of the little side rooms. As soon as they were inside the side room the blond said, "You know I haven't had a good hug all day. Can you fix that? Daniel?

Daniel gave the blond a big long hug. The blond said, "You look awful warm in that tie and buttoned up shirt. She began to unbutton Daniel's shirt. She placed both hands on his bare chest. She commented to Daniel, "Man you are harry." Daniel retorted, "No I am Daniel Harry is my brother in Florida." The blond laughed and sort of fell all over Daniel. Daniel put his arms around the blonds waste and kissed her on the lips. The blond said, "What would it take for you to sponsor a bill in Congress that would eliminate the restrictions on teen age alcohol? I mean you could tack it on to one of the appreciations bills. Is there anything I can do to convince you that this is a good idea? I am prepared to do most anything, Daniel." Daniel said, "Honey you are awful tempting but I just don't play that kind of game. He put his shirt back on and left the room.

EXCESSIVE GOVERNMENT REGULATIONS

Congressman Ferguson My name is Mrs. Hattie P. Moore. I have a complaint about excessive Government regulations. You may ask why I am complaining. Well, let me tell you. It all started in my kitchen about three years ago. I love to bake blueberry muffins for my Grandkids. Nevertheless, let me back up a bit.

I had just picked some fresh blueberries at a U-Pick blueberry farm. I was sure that the very fresh blueberries would make excellent blueberry muffins. I normally bake twelve muffins at a time but since I had so many blueberries I made twenty-four this time. I did not have room for all of these blueberry muffins so I stashed twelve of the muffins into a side storage cabinet. When the Four Grand Kids came over, four of the muffins just disappeared. On the next visit about a week later the rest of the twelve-pan container of muffins were all gone. It was a week after this that I remembered the twelve blueberry muffins that I had stashed away in the side cabinet.

Well these blueberry muffins were stale and did not have the soft spongy feel that fresh muffins should have. I hated to throw away these muffins so I tried one by dunking it into my coffee. Low and Behold. The crunchy feel of the coffee dunked blueberry muffin was delicious. I invited some friends over and they tried my stale blueberry muffins in some coffee. They said, "Hattie why do not you sell these muffins. They are great."

I made some more stale blueberry muffins and gave them to my neighbors. All of my neighbors said they wanted to purchase some blueberry muffins just like the ones they had tasted. I had people banging on my door wanting my stale blueberry muffins. In order to supply the demand I had to use a vegetable dehydrator to make the fresh blueberry muffins stale. My kitchen was too small to make all of the muffins I could sell. I rented an empty building and purchased three new ovens. A salesperson came by and talked me into purchasing printed boxes for my muffin sales. He said, "you need a good name for the muffins." We settled on, "Crusty Elite"

Within a week, I had to hire another cook to help me make sufficient Crusty Elite Stale Blueberry Muffins. I bought another oven and three more Kitchen-Aid Mixers.

A local store wanted me to supply Crusty Elite Blueberry Muffins to all twelve of their stores. I bought a used izzu delivery truck and painted it white. I got a local painter to stencil my Crusty Elite Blueberry Muffin LOGO on the side of the truck. A young neighbor offered to deliver the Crusty Elite Blueberry Muffins to the twelve stores.

Business was booming. I had money in the bank for the first time. The only problem I had was I could not make all of the Crusty Elite Blueberry Muffins that the market demanded well I thought that was my only problem.

The food inspectors came in and did a number on my baking facility. They wrote up twenty-seven violations of their food preparation code. I was told that I had thirty days to correct all of these violations or close the doors. Six of these violations are no problem as I intended to fix them even before the food inspectors arrived. There was no way I could fix half of the so-called problems. Crusty Elite Blueberry Muffins doors are shuttered. You see Mr. Congressman Ferguson Your Excessive Regulations has put me out of business. I have angry customers calling me every day wanting to know why. Mr. Congressman what shall I tell my angry customers?

Congressman Ferguson responded, "Miss Moore the Food service regulations were enacted to protect your customers. My suggestion is to fix the violations and continue to satisfy your customers

BLACK MOUNTAIN VILLAGE THM

Damon Wineseller remarked to the President, "The last Town Hall Meeting in Death Valley Dooms was a disaster. I am for giving it one more try before we give up on the idea. What say you Mr. President? The President replied, "Ok let's give it one better try." The Campaign Manager, Miss Nuddy Dancer, was called into the President's office and received her orders to set up a Town Hall Meeting in the little Mountain town called Black Mountain Village. The Campaign Manager said, "You guys want another Town Hall Meeting after the last fiasco in Death Valley Dooms. Wineseller said, "Yes, we are going to give it one more try."

Political Presidential Advisor, Damon Wineseller commented to the President, "Mr. President, It seems that a large number of voters are no longer elated by the historic novelty of your candidacy and are disappointed by your performance. I am afraid that voter turnout will be depressed this time. Mr. President to put it simple, you are in peril. I have just been informed that the Ames, Iowa Straw Poll indicates that a politically unknown young man, with lots of money, has emerged as a potential rival. This person is on a roll and will be hard to beat. I have a reliable report that the opposition has purchased eight hundred thousand front yard posters stating that, 'Our current President is a one term President.' These posters cost him $1.30 each. He just blew away over a million bucks.

We are going to have to do something and do it fast. We need some new thinking. I am not sure your new Campaign Manager, Miss Nuddy Dancer, is up to the task." The President retorted, "Mr. Wineseller I don't want to hear any more about Miss Nuddy Dancer and that is final." Damon Wineseller replied, "Understood Mr. President." The Town Hall Meeting was scheduled in the open High School football playing field. Radio, TV, and newspaper coverage was arranged by the Campaign Manager. Hand Bills were passes out. Posters were planted on every street corner.

The Presidents Town Hall Meeting was to be a big event. Free hot dogs and coke together with a scoop of vanilla ice cream and a cookie were offered to entice voters to attend.

One of the local politicians and mayor of Black Mountain Village hosted the meeting. Mayor Crapington brought the meeting to order about thirty minutes late. He gave the President a gracious introduction. He then asked for questions from the football playing field. A woman stepped to the microphone and introduced herself, "Mr. President my name is Mrs. Paige Turnner I am so glad you decided to visit our little village up here in the mountains. It seems to us that when the Government gives out any goodies it is the people living in the big towns that get the good stuff. We people living up here in the mountains get zilch. I realize that the town of Black Mountain Village can only give you a few votes and the big cities can deliver many more votes. However, I want you to bear in mind that when the voting is close every vote counts. It looks like the voting is going to be very close this election. Mr. President the town of Black Mountain Village did not receive one red cent of the fifty million dollar educational grant money. Our High School is in bad need of repair. We did not get any of the six million dollar un-wed mother grant money. There has been no effort on the federal Government's part to help our high un-employment. I see in the newspaper where the city of Detrott received 6 billion in unemployment help.

Our food kitchen is running very low on the essentials of life. I see where the Federal Government gave ten million pounds of wheat and 4 million pounds of sugar away from the food surplus program. We did not get a drop of it. Mr. President I know that you are here to muster some votes in the upcoming election.

May I suggest that you go to the big cities where you have helped so generously and seek some votes there? I am afraid you lost my vote several years ago. Thank you Mr. President for listening to me."

The President Responded to Mrs. Paige Turnner, "Thank you for your enlightening dissertation. I am so sorry to hear that your little community has been neglected by the Federal Government. I cannot correct the errors of the past but I will promise you that when I sign a bill from Congress from now on I will insist that the small villages like yours are included in the spoils."

The host Mayor Crapington asked for another question from the audience in football field. An elderly man stepped up to the microphone. He began, "Mr. President my name is Knoe Klass. A few months ago, I was at a cocktail party with some friends. One of my buddies commented, 'The Presidents shortcomings just cannot be fixed.' I dismissed his comment because he was known as an outspoken and defeated politician. As time marched on I have changed my mind and I agree with my outspoken political friend. I do not see how you can undo the mess you got us into. You have had four years now to straighten out the turmoil that the previous administration left you. I cannot see a single thing you have done to help our country or me.

There is an old saying that you should not fix something that is not broke. The only thing you tried to fix was not broke in the first place. Mr. President I know you came here in order to pick up some votes for the next election. I voted for you last time but you will not get my vote in the next election."

The President answered, "When I took office four years ago the country was not in great shape. Yes, I have had four years to straighten out the mess the previous administration left me. I can only do so much. Congress has blocked every attempt I have tried to make towards fixing the problems the previous administration shoved upon me. Mr. Klass, I thank you for your vote four years ago and I am so sorry that you cannot see the progress my administration had made in the last four years. I am truly regretful that I will not get your vote in the next election."

This time a man stepped up to the microphone. He said, "Mr. President My name is Deryls Perrials. I have a concern about our returning war veterans.

When we make the decision to go to War, we must take a hard look at the cost of this action. Let us suppose that the average pay per soldier from Generals on down to the buck privates is $ 5,000.00 per month. Suppose we send thirty thousand combat troops to the front lines. We need another 45 thousand support soldiers. The seventy-five thousand soldiers will consume 375,000,000.00 per month in base pay. Now we need ten helicopters, one hundred armored vehicles, fifty supply trucks, twenty-five oil/gasoline mobile tankers, a supply station, and a field hospital. Let us add up the cost so far:

Soldier's base pays .... $ 375,000,000.00 per month
Non-Expendable Expenses .... $ 81,970,000.00 per month
Expendable Expenses .... $ 30,000,000.00 per month
Total .... $ 486,970,000.00 per month

These figures do not include Variable Expenses like the cost of ammunition, repair parts, gasoline, clothing etc.

As you can see, the war is getting very expensive. However, hold on we are not through yet. Remember one of the items above is a field hospital. In a war, the enemy is shooting live ammunition at you.

Soldiers enter the field hospital with body parts missing, severe burns broken bones and mental conditions that are hard to describe. Take a poor country boy fresh from the farm and place him in front of a bunch of people shooting at him. He was able to cope with rattlesnakes, Mule kicks; Goat bumps, Chain saw cuts, and the like. However, grown men shooting at you are a different story. Many of the returning soldiers have some degree of mental illness. These Mental and physical conditions must be addressed. Cost? Who knows?

When we take a civilian and make a soldier out of him, we give him weeks of training to cope with his new life. When a soldier returns to civilian life, do we train the soldier to cope with his new civilian life? No! He is still warm and he will probably grow out of his mental illness.

My point is this; if you are prepared to go to war, you must be prepared to pay for all of the involved expenses. We must take care of our veterans. This expense must be one of the first considerations when figuring the cost of the war. You might even consider if the war is even worth it.

Mr. President, Your administration, and those before you have not fully addresses the returning veteran problem. You ask a soldier to put his life on the front line for his country; however, you turn your head when he comes home wounded. I mean wounds physically and mentally."

The President responded, "Mr. Perrials I thought we were doing a good job in the field of the returning veterans. You point out some very interesting facts that I will address when I return To DC. Although I disagree with your figures your presentation was outstanding. Thank you again Mr. Perrials."

Host Mayor Crapington asked for another question from the audience in the high school football field. Another man stepped forward and stood in front of the microphone. He said, "Mr. President my name is Mr. Oscar Fire Tree. I want to welcome you to our little town of Black Mountain Village. When you leave our village and drive north on the freeway you will see our National Forest on the right or east side of the freeway. There are many species of hard wood trees in the national forest. We have oak, walnut, apple, cherry and other hardwood trees there. We have several species if pine or evergreen trees there. The National Forest is beautiful. When it rains the mushrooms pop up and us Native Americans harvest them.

On the west or left hand, side of the freeway is the L'Pokono Indian reservation. The Sand Creek Band of the L'Pokono Indian tribe came from a renegade group of dissatisfied Native Americans that left the government provided Indian reservation in Oklahoma. The Sand Creek Band was not pleased with the confinement and restrictions placed upon the tribe in the Oklahoma reservation. The Sand Creek Band of the L'Pokono tribe fist tried to settle in Sand Creek. These were no jobs to be had for Native American in Sand Creek. The Sand Creek Band moved to the Black Mountain Area where they could find work. The tribe was about ten thousand strong at that time. That was before oil was discovered on the Oklahoma reservation. Many of the residents in Black Mountain Village are originally from the L'Pokono Indian reservation. There are very little jobs on the reservation so we come to the Village to live and work.

We are all happy in our little town of Black Mountain Village. Mr. President my request to you is please remember Black Mountain Village and The L'Pokono Indian Reservation the next time you dole out the goodies from DC. With that, I thank you very much."

The President responded, "Mr. Firetree I certainly will remember Black Mountain Village and the L'Pokono Indian

Reservation not only when money is disbursed from DC but the friendly faces here are a good thing to remember."

Host Mayor Crapington asked for another question from the High School Football Field Audience. An elderly woman made her way up to the microphone podium. She began to speak into the microphone, "Mr. President I want to thank you for the good job you are doing It must be an awesome feeling to know that you have the responsibility as the chief executive officer of these United States of America In addition to that you are the Commander-in-Chief of our armed forces. The pressure of these responsibilities may seem unbearable at times. Again, Thank you Mr. President.

Mr. President my name is Mrs. Monica Kaputin. I began my work life when I was twenty years old. For forty-five years, I cleaned the office buildings at night after the office workers went home to their families. I retired at age sixty-five. My only source of income is the Social Security check I receive each month. I have to rely upon Medicare for my health insurance. In the latest rounds of budget cuts, you and Congress are cutting back on the Social Security Payments and decreasing the coverage under Medicare.

Now when I get sick I have to pay more for my health care out of a decreased Social Security check. I am being hit with a double whammy. Mr. President I am in a box from which I cannot escape. I want you to please look at the Social Security and Medicare cuts and see what you are doing to older

Citizens like me. I have bad arthritis and I can no longer work at my old job. Thank you Mr. President for listening to me."

The President responded to Mrs. Monica Kaputin's request, "Mrs. Kaputin there are hundreds of thousand if not millions women with financial situations just like yours.

We must curb the national debt. We must decrease government spending. Many entitlement programs must be cut back. Social Security and Medicare are the biggest burden on the federal government's budget. We must make these cuts."

Mrs. Monica Kaputin countered, "Yes, I understand the need to cut back on the entitlement programs. Mr. President Social Security is not an entitlement. It was and still is funded by the working people."

The President Continued, "My suggestion to you is to cut out some of the frills that you can afford to lose. You like the Federal Government must learn to live within our budgets."

A few boos were heard coming from the very back of the High School Football Playing Field.

Host, Mayor Crapington, sensed that the crowd may turn ugly so he announced the close of the Town Hall Meeting. In addition, we all stood and sang the National Anthem.

FORT KAPUT THM

The President called Mr. Damon Wineseller and Miss Nuddy Dancer into his office for an emergency meeting. The President announced, "I have ten letters in my hand from some troops in Fort Kaput. It seems that the returning veterans have some concerns that need to be addressed. The military vote is going to be important in November. I want to be on the good side with these boys.

I know that our past Town Hall Meetings have been very disappointing. As Commander-in-Chief of the Armed Forces, I think I have a little clout. Miss Nuddy Dancer I want you to set up a Town Hall Meeting in Fort Kaput as soon as possible."

Miss Nuddy Dancer had no problem arraigning the Town Hall Meeting at Fort Kaput. Master Sergeant Ruby Dhou. Was appointed host for the meeting.

Host Master Sergeant Ruby Dhou introduced the President and Commander-in-Chief of the Armed Forces. She thanked the President for paying a visit to the Fort. The President made a very short campaign speech. The host asked for questions from the audience. A young corporal raised his hand. The host pointed towards the corporal and said, "it's all yours corporal." The Corporal said, "Mr. President, my name is Joseph Rodriguez. I just came back from Afkanstamp. What I do not understand is why we were not allowed to win the war and get it over in a hurry. We are the most powerful nation in the world. We act like a third world poverty nation when it comes to war. We could have blown those people off the map.

We did not choose to take this action. Instead, we just lagged along and lost a great number of our finest men. What say you, Mr. President?" The President responded, "That is a good question Corporal. I have heard that comment several times before now. We need to take a serious look at our war policy. I will take your comments under advisement. Thank you Corporal."

The host Master Sergeant Ruby Dhou asked for another question from the audience. A buck sergeant stood up and he was recognized by the host. The Sergeant said, "Mr. President my name is Roy Smith. I also just returned to the U. S. from Afkanstamp. I could not find a civilian job on the outside so I reenlisted for another six years in the Army. Mr. President why do not you give the returning vets a break in the hiring of federal workers?"

The President responded, "A very good question Sergeant Smith. I will have my Secretary of Labor look into this."

The host Master sergeant Ruby Dhou asked for another question from the audience. A young woman recruit raised her hand and she was recognized by the host. The new recruit began, "Mr. President, My name is Louise Crabb. We have a fair number of women in the armed services. I have noticed that the higher you go in rank the fewer women are present. I would like to see us women treated equally with the male military population." The President responded, "The rules and regulations that govern the promotion of qualified solders do not reference the sex of the candidate. If these rules and regulations are not followed then you have recourse through the Inspector General's Office."

The Host said, we have time for one more question then the President will have to go back to DC. An older soldier stood up and he was recognized by the host. "Mr. President, My name is Sergeant Jones. I have been in the Army for nineteen years. I fear the day that I will be discharged into the civilian world. When I came into the Army from civilian life, you gave me plenty of training to help me adjust to Army life. There is no training for soldiers to help them adjust to civilian life." The President answered, "You are right sergeant Jones. This area needs to be looked into. I will bring this up with the Secretary of Defense when I get back to DC."

The host Master Sergeant Ruby Dhou thanked the President for his very short visit to Fort Kaput. The President said it was a pleasure being here and he hoped to return soon.

THE CONCEEDING FAREWELL PARTY

The President and his new Campaign Management Staff worked hard for the next two months. Every effort was measured for effectiveness and costs. Changes were made frequently to adjust to the new pole findings. Speeches were written and rewritten to try to please the majority of the voters. The President kept constant pressure on his new Campaign Manager, Miss Nuddy Dancer. Every member of the President's team knew he was serious. Each member of the team made an all-out effort.

After all of the blood, sweat and tears, election day finally rolled around.

The President and his Cabinet, His Campaign Team, and key members of his political party all sat in front of a huge 98-inch HD TV screen. The round office was full of people. At 6:00PM DC time, the news forecasters began to guess at the election outcome. Two predicted defeat for the President. Three newscasters gave the President a good chance. At seven in the evening, some of the east coast poles closed. The guessing game was now three against the President and two for the President. At seven-thirty big maps of the United States began to show how the voters in each State decided. At eight in the evening most of the East Coast States had counted their votes. It did not look good. Five States for the President and eleven for the opposition. Nine in the evening closed all of the poles except for the West Coast States. The tally was now eighteen for the President and twenty-eight for the opposition. The Midwestern States where the President was the strongest did not make that much difference. At ten PM, all poles were closed and the final tally on the big screen was twenty-one for the President and thirty-one for the opposition.

At eleven PM, the President made his Conceding speech written by one of his new speechwriters. After making his conceding speech, he turned to his fellow workers and said, "Well that is it. I think this calls for a party at THE GREY HIUSE DC. We are going to have one hell of a farewell party." He looked at Lori-Ann and said, "you heard it let us get things rolling for our farewell party." As the President looked across the room, he could see tear eyed teammates trying to hide their sorrow in white handkerchiefs. He said to them, "I am sorry I let you down. I wish I could make it easier for you but I cannot." A big tear was seen to roll down the President's cheek and fall to the floor. The President was more concerned about the feelings of others than the hurt down deep inside him.

Lori-Ann called the President and said there is not enough money to have a decent farewell party. The President said to Lori-Ann, "Call that Lobbyist Hammon Bacon that represents the Liquor industry and tell him that we are having a farewell party. We need some Booze." Hammon Bacon's response to Lori-Ann is that he could only supply two cases of cheap tequila. He further said he could not ride a losing horse. I will send the liquor over but my girls and I will not be there for the party. Lori-Ann tried several contacts that were all willing to help when things were going great. A different story is heard when you are down. Lori-Ann said to one of her coworkers, "It's a dog eat dog world out there nobody wants to help you when you are down. I do not know how I am going to put together a party with no money and no friends." Lori-Ann is a fighter. She kept plugging away until she had a decent party planned.

At 7:00PM, the three-piece band started to play. First, to arrive at the farewell party was Bula Klinginghouse followed by Dee Dee and Kan Kan Bowman. Senator Isenhardt and Congressmen Epstein his wife Linda were next to arriving. It was not long before Congressmen Christopher, Daniel Bachelor, Miller, Nelson, and Ferguson showed up. The three-piece band would play two numbers and take a break then back for two more numbers. The guitar player forgot his electric guitar tuner and he was off key somewhat. The keyboard player only knew three chords or the tree chords were his favorites. Hammon Bacon said he would not attend but he showed up anyway. He sought out Lori-Ann and apologized being so rude on the phone. He saw the party was going to be flop so he offered to supply some more free booze. This time Hammon brought in the good stuff and plenty of it. More Senators and Congressmen drifted in as time went on. At 9:00 PM, the house was almost full. Booz was flowing freely. People were drinking to this and that. Some were paring off and a lot of hugging and kissing was going on. This would be their last party at THE GREY HOUSE DC. The next President was much older than out person and it is rumored that he does not like to party. The President left the party at 1:00AM. He said he was tired and went to bed. The Farewell party lasted until about 2:30 AM.

Just before going to sleep, the President said to his wife, "Honey, It has been a hard four years and I am kind of glad it is over. She wiped away a big tear she felt on his cheek as she kissed him goodnight.

THE END